Acclaim for the Debut Novel of BRIAN DE PALMA and SUSAN LEHMAN!

"*Are Snakes Necessary?* is brilliant, lurid, twisty fun. Working together, Susan Lehman and Brian De Palma have captured in print something akin to one of De Palma's dreamlike visual masterpieces. Compulsively readable and fiendishly constructed."
> —*David Koepp, screenwriter of Mission: Impossible, Jurassic Park, and Spider-Man*

"A deliciously deceptive novel…The writing is nearly pitch-perfect…When the surprises start to come, one after another, with increasing rapidity, we realize there have been a few subplots running behind the scenes, just out of our view, that have suddenly become visible, altering the whole texture of the novel. A wonderful, immensely satisfying thriller."
> —*Booklist*

"A clever thriller and a brilliant charge against American politicians."
> —*Le Figaro*

"The supercharged grace of James Ellroy's L.A. *Confidential* with less despair and more humor."
> —*Marianne*

"A great first novel, a beautiful discovery."
> —*Read*

The sun is still bright, dagger bright, when Nick pulls the blue Cutlass into Elizabeth's long circular driveway, the one that leads to Diamond's glass castle in the desert. Bruce opens the door.

"Come on in, homewrecker," he tells Nick. "Come to say your goodbyes? The missus will be down shortly. Meanwhile can I pour you a farewell drink?"

Though entirely unnerved, Nick plays it cool. Mostly because he has no idea what else to do. The house looks like a place James Bond would feel at home.

Bruce takes the bottle he is carrying and unscrews the top. He goes over to the bar to get some water and ice cubes and makes two Scotches on the rocks. He lifts his drink to Nick.

"Well, well, you surprised me. I didn't think you went in for this kind of cheesy stuff. Fucking the boss's wife. Pretty ballsy."

Nick finds it harder to play it cool. "At least I don't beat her."

Bruce laughs. Too hard. He follows this with an alligator grin. "How wrong you are..."

Are Snakes Necessary?

by **Brian De Palma**
and **Susan Lehman**

A HARD CASE CRIME NOVEL

A HARD CASE CRIME BOOK

(HCC-144)

First Hard Case Crime edition: March 2020

Published by

Titan Books
A division of Titan Publishing Group Ltd
144 Southwark Street
London SE1 0UP

in collaboration with Winterfall LLC

Print edition ISBN 978-1-78909-120-5
E-book ISBN 978-1-78909-121-2

Design direction by Max Phillips
www.maxphillips.net

Typeset by Swordsmith Productions

The name "Hard Case Crime" and the Hard Case Crime logo are trademarks of Winterfall LLC. Hard Case Crime books are selected and edited by Charles Ardai.

Printed in the United States of America

Visit us on the web at www.HardCaseCrime.com

ARE SNAKES NECESSARY?

CHAPTER 1

Barton Brock had a bad day. A very bad day.

The vasectomy was not, as the doctor promised, painless. Brock's balls hurt and he is having unpleasant thoughts about swelling, discoloration and perpetual soreness.

This is not the worst of it. The poll numbers are devastating. It looks like Jason Crump is going to get creamed. The primary is just four weeks away.

"Fuck, fuck, fuck." These are pretty much the only words going through Barton Brock's head. It's Brock's job to get Crump elected, and he can't fuck up.

Political campaigns are brutal. The stakes are high. Not for the electorate—Barton Brock does not particularly care about the electorate. But for the team, the one that boosts the candidate into office, the stakes matter, a lot. The guys on the team get big payoffs, good appointments, cushy jobs, bigger campaigns.

It's like fishing. You start small, then throw away the little guys, the ones self-respecting cats wouldn't call dinner—and then you cast out for the big mothers.

Crump's big problem is that he's up against Lee Rogers, mister fancy-pants incumbent who's scared off most of the challengers in Pennsylvania's Republican primary.

Crump, an Iraq war vet who has a chest full of medals and an artificial leg to show for his trouble in Operation Desert Storm, does not lack for candidate brownie points. And he has a nice, yes-you-*would*-like-to-have-a-beer-with-this-guy frat-boy appeal.

The trouble is he doesn't have a lot going on upstairs. Certainly nothing Rogers, with his Columbia Law School dazzle, can't blow away at the debate in two weeks.

As Crump's campaign manager and strategist, Brock's MO springs from a line he read in a David Mamet play: "The only way to teach these guys a lesson is to kill them."

Brock *is* going to teach the pretty-boy politicos a great big lesson, one that will kill their chances. And it's going to take a very dirty trick to do it.

Brock, 42 and busily *not* thinking about how he is *not* going to tell his wife about the vasectomy, applies himself to the question of how best to smear Senator Rogers.

First thing, we move the news cycle away from foreign policy, farm subsidies and all that and towards something Rogers would rather not talk about, something like his zipper problem, maybe.

Brock feels a familiar excitement as he considers what dirty rabbit he can pull out of his hat. Suspecting that Dr. Jack Daniels might supply a little inspiration, Brock drives his rental sedan past several hard-to-distinguish strip malls—it seems to Brock that suburban Pennsylvania may, in fact, be one interconnected strip mall. He steers the sedan into a big lot and heads towards One Fish, Two Fish, a tavern at strip's end. A swollen goldfish floats at the top of the tank inside the front door. Brock pulls a stool up to the bar and orders. A couple of shots later, no light bulbs have gone off.

The good thing about having a history, even a bad history, is that your record can be a source of confidence—or sometimes supply a sense of direction. Brock, now dim in the ideas department, decides maybe a little sleep will kickstart his dark genius. He'll come up with something in the morning. He's sure he will. He always has.

He heads for the Red Roof Inn Motel, and, just before the turn-off, is cheered by the sight of a pair of golden arches. McDonald's. God Bless America and God Bless late-night snacks.

Brock ducks inside. It's a few minutes before closing. A sur-real vision greets him at the counter: there stands a drop-dead gorgeous blonde. Her stiff yellow apron barely contains her voluptuous curves. For a moment Brock imagines a wrestling match between her giant breasts and the tight seams of her Ronald McDonald wear. His better ball starts to tingle.

"Double quarter pounder with cheese."

"Anything extra?" asks the knockout.

"Just one question."

"Is the answer on the menu?"

"Nope. It's a personal question."

The blonde shakes her head. She's beat.

"Sorry, mister. I've been on my feet for twelve hours. I'm ready to go home. If it's not on the menu, I'm not interested in what you have on your mind."

"Really? How about this: I wonder if you'd be interested in a better-paying job that doesn't require you to be on your feet all day."

Elizabeth deCarlo looks up at the clock. She looks back at Brock. He seems a little rough around the edges but he's got on a suit and tie and looks like he could be some kind of manager. He does not look scary.

Ten minutes later, Elizabeth has turned off the blinding dining area lights and is sitting inside Brock's nondescript black town car.

Brock gets right to the point.

"I'm the campaign manager for Jason Crump. We need people to conduct push polls tomorrow."

"Push polls?"

Brock explains that push polling involves calling Republicans, encouraging them to go to the polls and slipping in a few ques-tions before they hang up the phone.

"What kind of questions?" Elizabeth doesn't quite follow and wants to go home.

"Like how do they feel about their candidate supporting Right-to-Life legislation?"

"That's it?"

"That's it."

"What does it pay?"

Brock knows push polling doesn't pay anything. Local volunteers do this stuff for nothing. But he has an idea it would be good to have Elizabeth in his sphere of influence where he can prime her for a job she was born to play, one that will be extremely lucrative.

Ten days in and $2,000 later, Brock calls Elizabeth into his office for a special after-hours chat.

"How's the job going?"

Elizabeth shrugs. "Most of the people I talk to don't know who Jason Crump is. In fact they don't even know they're supposed to vote next month. They *do* know who Senator Rogers is."

"They bring his name up?"

"Yep."

"How do they feel about his womanizing?"

"I don't ask them about that. Am I missing something?"

"Rogers has a history of philandering."

"Stop the presses," she says. "What man hasn't? And what difference does it make? Aren't we campaigning for Crump?"

Brock affects a professorial tone. Political Campaigning 101. "We are. But one way to campaign for Crump is to attack Rogers, expose his negatives."

In a matter of seconds, Brock unveils his big idea. "This is a man who plays around, okay? He's been doing it for years. He just hasn't been caught. The voters deserve to know the truth about the man representing them in Washington, don't you think?"

Elizabeth doesn't care much one way or the other.

Brock continues. "How about this. We get the senator in a compromising position with a girl and photograph it. Maybe we send a couple copies around, stir up some gossip with a little strategically placed web video. Then we push poll along these lines: 'Lee Rogers cheats on his wife. Would this make you more likely or less likely to vote for him?' "

Brock smiles. It's simple. It will be deadly. He'll be that much closer to the Crump victory that is his job.

Elizabeth gets it. "Sounds like a pretty dirty trick."

"Exactly. And it's kind of an ideal smear. It will cause a ruckus and no one will be able to trace it back to the Crump campaign."

Brock has been studying Elizabeth's cleavage for the past few moments. He's not subtle. So Elizabeth isn't surprised when he says, "You're going to be the girl in the photograph. You know, the heart of the dirty little rumor."

"I don't think so, Mr. Brock. Thank you very much but I'm going back to my job at McDonald's."

Greasy french fries, dirty tricks, it all sounds pretty much the same to Elizabeth. She doesn't need to get involved in political smearing. Big Macs are oily enough.

"Sit down!" Brock barks. Now this guy is beginning to scare her. Elizabeth sits back down. "You think minimum wage at McDonald's is going to pay for you to fight that nasty landlord who is trying to evict you from your home?"

"What do you know about that? That's my personal business."

"I'm concerned about the welfare of my employees. I try to be well acquainted with their personal problems. And you need money. A lot of it. Even bad lawyers are expensive." Brock has a sinister cool. He's got it all figured out.

Elizabeth knows when her back is to the wall. She does need money. Fuck. Maybe this sneaky bastard can help. *She's* not running for Senate. How compromising can it be?

"Okay," she says. "Let's cut to the chase. You want Rogers to be caught with someone just like me."

Brock smiles. "You are a bright girl."

"How much?"

"Ten grand."

"Make it fifteen. And throw in a couple of grand for a clothes budget. I can't go to work dressed like this."

CHAPTER 2

Elizabeth's new job is easy. Much easier than flipping burgers.

She sits at the bar at the Boody House Hotel. The one where Lee Rogers is staying.

She wears jeans and a creamy silk blouse. Elizabeth knows a bit about fashion and sex appeal. It's the flash of skin, the point where the conceal and reveal join, that is most interesting. This is a fancy way of saying that her blouse is buttoned to the third button. Discreet but inviting.

Guess who accepts the invitation? Yes. Lee Rogers.

He walks in after a staff meeting, thinks about going to his room, sees 19-year-old Elizabeth at the bar and turns around.

"Hi there," he says with practiced charm.

"Buy a girl a drink?"

When you really get down to it, it's not so hard to get things moving. A few Manhattan swigs later, Elizabeth is twirling the cherry stem on her tongue and trying out her favorite dumb Southern bunny accent.

"Oh Senator, my Lord, is it really you? Do you know that I helped my mama cast a vote for you when I was just a little girl? She took me in the booth with her and let me pull the lever. I know you're the only one who keeps us safe from all those terrible terrorists. I'm so looking forward to the debate on Sunday with that, he's practically a communist, that liberal Crummy or whatever his name is. Would I like to see how you prepare for a debate? Right now? Upstairs in your suite? I would be honored."

The next morning Elizabeth walks into Brock's office. "Check this out," she says looking like the Cheshire Cat as she offers Brock a selfie that shows her lying naked next to the sleeping senator. She's carefully framed the photo so her face is cut off but her body doesn't lie.

Brock is very pleased. Elizabeth was a good hire.

Brock tells her to meet his paymaster in the McDonald's parking lot that evening.

Brock keeps his eyes on Elizabeth's bottom as she walks out of the office and closes the door behind her. Then Brock gets up, follows her out the door and takes off towards Rogers' hotel.

It's early morning. Brock, a real pro, is of course familiar with Rogers' schedule and knows that the senator will be in his room working on debate prep.

A yawning Senator Rogers opens the door in a bathrobe.

"Well hello, Mr. Brock. What brings you here so early? Come to concede the election already?"

"Morning, Senator. Nope. Not here to concede. But I do have something I think you'll find interesting. May I come in?"

"Please, please," says Rogers, who exudes almost unnatural delight at the appearance of his rival's top operative. "Always a pleasure to see what the opposition has dreamt up. Your push polling has been very instructive."

Brock is all business. Though he has something like a mental hard-on as he anticipates Rogers' reaction to the photo, which Brock holds up on the screen of his iPhone as soon as he's inside the senator's room.

Rogers leans back against the hotel room desk and just smiles. "I guess I'll be seeing this on *Washington Whispers* as soon as you leave. Or maybe it's already there?"

"No, Senator, the picture isn't on *Washington Whispers*...yet. And it could vanish entirely, if *you* concede the election. I understand your wife has been diagnosed with Parkinson's. Don't you think this might be a good time to put your political ambitions aside and go home and look after that magnificent lady?"

Rogers laughs in Brock's face.

Brock is uncomfortable. Has Rogers gone mad? Or has Brock? Having someone laugh at you brings back memories of early childhood and some of its worst horrors.

"I'm surprised at you, Brock. Pulling a cheap trick like this. Go ahead. Upload your naughty picture. I'll deny it of course. And when it's analyzed and discovered to be a fake, guess whose doorstep the media is going to be parked on?"

"It's not a fake, Senator. It was taken right here in this hotel room."

"You sure, Brock? Do you really want to bet your political career on that?"

Brock can feel the weight of pennies dropping from his eyes and he doesn't like it at all. He can't place it exactly but he definitely has the feeling he's been taken somehow. He rifles through the options in his mind and sees quickly he has no choice but to play this out.

"Fake? Why do you say that?"

Rogers smiles. Actually it's more of a grin. The haughty grin of a winner who gets that it would be impolite to smile at a man he's just beaten. "Because we faked it. You know Photoshop, right? Amazing little program. You just push a few buttons. Use the blur tool around the collarbone. It's my face on another body next to Elizabeth's."

Temporary loss of composure on Brock's side of the room. *"You did this together?"*

"If a whore can be bought once, she can be bought twice. Oops! I wasn't supposed to tell you about our little deal until you paid her off."

"Fuck, fuck, fuck" are the only words going through Brock's mind.

Rogers is having fun. "By the way, have you looked at the polling this morning?"

Brock nods. His candidate is 30 points behind.

"Brock. Face facts. There is no way that Crump is going to win this primary. You know it. I know it. I quite enjoyed meeting your friend last night. We had a lot of fun creating this picture. It gets real boring on the campaign trail."

Brock has been outfoxed. He shoves the phone with the photo into his pocket and starts for the door.

"Hold on a minute."

Brock stops and turns to face Rogers.

"Crump is a loser," says Rogers. "But I appreciate a man of your inventiveness. Why don't you throw in the towel on that guy. Along with everyone else. How about coming to work for me?"

There is something of the fait accompli in the air even as the words leave Rogers' lips. If a whore can be bought once, she can be bought twice.

Elizabeth drives into McDonald's later that night. She's here to collect the fifteen thousand Brock promised. True, she's already collected twenty from Rogers, for changing sides, and that's nice—but she's got bills to pay. Plus she likes the idea of collecting from both sides.

She looks around the lot and is surprised to find it empty, except for a police car. The one that's often there, two fat cops inside munching Big Macs, "patrolling the premises."

One of the officers sees Elizabeth drive up; he watches as she looks around and then makes eye contact with a man in a suit. The suit walks towards her.

"Do you work for Barton Brock?"

"Yes," says the suit.

"Do you have the money?"

The suit pulls a brown bag from under his jacket and hands it to Elizabeth. She opens it up and peeks inside. Fat banded stacks of cash. Just like in the movies.

Reveling in the sight of all that money, Elizabeth doesn't

notice when one of the officers gets out of his car and walks towards her. But she definitely hears him when, holding a badge in front of her face, he says, "Don't move, ma'am. You're under arrest."

Brock, who really hates to be outfoxed, is a tricky dog. He's gone an extra mile to make sure Elizabeth is charged with solicitation and blackmail and that the charges stick. Bail is out of the question. Worse, it all hits as she's about to enter into the grueling eviction battle that could leave her without a home. She hears about Rogers' landslide in the TV room/smoking lounge at the minimum-security facility in Crawford County where she's sentenced to a 36-month term.

A few weeks after she hears the news of Rogers' victory, a not unfriendly guard tells Elizabeth she has a visitor.

Elizabeth sits in a bare visitation cell wondering who is coming to visit. She looks charming in her prison suit and, in a way, resembles Piper Kerman, though Elizabeth's suit is gray and not orange. Is she surprised when the guard approaches, keys jangling, with Barton Brock? Yes, but she doesn't let on.

Brock is all business as usual. He wants Elizabeth out of town. He won't look good—and neither will his new boss, Senator Lee Rogers—if people start asking questions. If Elizabeth can be bought twice, no telling how many other buyers out there might find her story interesting. Brock figures if he sends her out of town, far out of town, with a little cash in her pocket, he can buy her silence. "How would you like to get out of here?" he says.

"You double-crossing motherfucker."

"Look at the pot calling the kettle black. Calm down. Politics is a dirty business. We're going to get you off the playing field as quickly as possible."

This is not a game for Elizabeth. She starts to cry. Not the kind of tears women sometimes deploy in emergency situations (when tears are both unstoppable and also useful), but genuine tears. Misery made liquid. "I lost my home."

"Sorry about that. But you shouldn't have tried to fuck me." Brock holds up a hand, palm out, when he sees something like anger spark behind her eyes. "I'm not the kind of a guy to hold a grudge. I think you've learned your lesson. I had a talk with the DA, he's going to drop all the charges if…"

"If what." Quiet tears continue to fall down Elizabeth's cheeks.

"…you disappear from here and never return. I got you a bus ticket to Las Vegas. One way. I have a friend in the Diamond organization who will give you a job in one of his casinos. All you have to do in return is shut up. Forever. Forget everything about the Rogers campaign."

"You fucker, you think you can destroy people's lives and get away with it."

Brock slaps her hard. She falls back into her chair. The guard looks out the window as if something truly amazing is going on just outside the barred glass.

"Lady, take the ticket, while I'm feeling generous. I could have you sliced and diced in here and no one…" He motions to the guard who is still transfixed by the something, nothing, about the tree outside the window. "…would do one fucking thing to stop it."

Brock reaches inside his jacket and hands her the ticket. It is very hard for Elizabeth to look even slightly dignified as she bows her head and takes it. But she does. Elizabeth has an innate grace. And now she has a get out of jail free card in her pocket.

CHAPTER 3

Lee Rogers, still flush from victory, marches through the San Francisco airport.

Another "ideas conference," another $50K check. Yum.

A kitchen. Maybe the senator will give the money to the missus so she can do that kitchen renovation she's been nattering about.

Fuck. It's been a long season on the campaign trail.

Maybe, thinks Rogers, *I'll get this dog a little treat.*

Rogers and Brock march towards the baggage claim.

Brock, inexhaustible, raises the question of Rogers' position on fracking.

"Got to take into account those upstate voters, Senator. Might want to schedule a meet-and-greet up in Pittsburgh. Some badly ruffled feathers up there. Show a little love and we could sock up some early support from Atlas Energy."

Yawn. Not a bad idea, but Rogers is a little busy right now, thank you, eyeing the skirt in front of him. *Nice ass*, he thinks.

Nice ass stops, checks her watch.

Squeak squeak. Nice ass has those rubber-soled shoes, the kind stewardesses wear. They squeak when she starts walking.

Rogers focuses in. Skirt nice and tight. The way he likes. But prim. Crisp blouse. *Wait a minute*, Rogers thinks, registering the uniform. *Isn't that the Loft Air outfit?*

Loft Air! Squeak! Rogers' heart races.

Could it be? Jenny, Jenny, Jenny…oh what was her last name? Jenny Cours! That's it!

Why do we never forget the ones that got away? Rogers

quickens his pace. And, eyes trained on her ass, he catches up with Jenny Cours.

She is dark haired and slim and may, in truth, be one of very few people on earth who actually looks good in air hostess garb. Better than good, really. Jenny Cours looks really good, very good, for her age.

(Why do they say that? Couldn't they just leave it at Jenny Cours looks good? But no, they can't. Jenny, at 47, appealing as she is, is also at the age at which "for her age" is the dark coda added to all complimentary remarks.)

To Rogers the fact that older women bear a certain extra burden is as relevant as the upstate farmer who got a bum deal from the frackers and whose faucet releases poisonous—and also flammable—water whenever he turns the spigot on. Jenny Cours looks fucking fantastic to him; his blood races at the memory of a pleasant heat.

"Jenny! Jenny Cours, I can't believe it's you!" Rogers, in a spruce black suit and Zegna tie, has the disposition of a puppy who has been in the cargo compartment on a long flight.

"Lee!" Big smile. "How long has it been?" Jenny Cours is cucumber cool, but definitely not unfriendly.

"Twenty years. It's been twenty years. Wow, oh wow. Jenny Cours!"

Jenny smiles. "You look well, Lee."

"Fantastic! You look *fantastic*, Jenny." The senator beams. Suddenly he remembers his old nickname for her. "Jen Jen. What have you been doing all this time? Still flying, I see?"

Know this about Jenny Cours. She may be the last happy person on earth. She has lots of grace and poise and, though she was not class valedictorian or anything—not by a long shot— she left high school with a clear sense of who she is, bright, capable, ready, and full of life. Jenny Cours likes who she is, thank you very much.

She knew early on that she wanted to fly and here she is, an air hostess on Loft Airlines, where she's worked for over twenty years.

Flying all over the world sounds exciting and there are ways in which it definitely is—Milan for dinner! London for lunch! It gets routine after a time, but in a comfortable, soothing way that Jenny has come to like.

"Still flying, Lee. Just came in from Paris with a layover in New York. I've been living in Menlo Park and boy am I glad to get home and have a hot bath and get to bed nice and early."

Talk of bath and bed warms Rogers' heart and he is about to pull a line or two from his practiced ladykiller repertoire when a tornado of youthful energy bounds up. "Hi, Mom!" says the tornado. Perkily and without self-consciousness, the young girl at the center of the storm hugs Jenny in her slender arms.

"Fanny! What are you doing here?"

In her sudden focus on her young daughter, Jenny has all but forgotten Lee Rogers; this the senator registers with annoyance.

"Can't a girl come out to meet her mom?"

Fanny, 18, is in the full flush of carnality. Neither her vitality and ripeness nor the irrepressible sense of readiness that surrounds her elude the impatient senator.

"Oh, sweetheart, of course she can!" says Jenny, returning her daughter's great big hug.

Fanny explains she thought she'd meet her mom's plane and surprise her since school is out. "And what do I find?" says Fanny, eyeing the senator and flashing a great big toothsome smile at him. "You chatting with the biggest landslide victor in recent senatorial history?"

Fanny is a political junkie. Unlike her friends, self-respecting 18-year-olds who spend weekends in bed, binge watching *Shameless* and *Pretty Little Liars*, Fanny can't get enough of politics. She surfs the web for political news, analysis, debate and gossip and may be the youngest member of the senior set who tune into the Sunday news shows.

Jenny is so excited by Fanny's surprise appearance she's forgotten to introduce Lee Rogers.

"I'm sorry. Lee, this is my daughter, Fanny. Fanny, meet the senior senator from Pennsylvania. Lee Rogers."

"My pleasure," says Fanny, extending her arm and holding Lee Rogers' hand tight in hers. "What you did in the campaign, with your media strategy, when Crump ran his attack ads..."

"The pleasure is all mine. I had no idea Jen Jen had such a...vibrant, enthusiastic, *knowledgeable* daughter!"

Brock, who has been patiently standing (lurking might be more like it) behind the senator, decides it's time to wrap up the airport reunion and get the show on the road. Neither the kid nor her analysis of the Crump campaign and the commercials in which he clunked forth on a steel leg could be less interesting to Brock. In fact, Brock registers some alarm at Lee's interest in this little pop tart and the aging mom.

But Rogers is in no hurry to go anywhere. Except perhaps for a drink with Jenny Cours and her lovely daughter. "Hold your fire, Chief," he tells Brock.

Jenny, however, is entirely with Brock in thinking it's time to wrap up and get out of here.

"Let's hit the road, my dear," Jenny tells Fanny, prompted by visions of a nice mother–daughter reunion complete with kale salad and chardonnay followed by that bath and bed. Jenny looks at her watch, grabs Lee's hand and gives it a shake. "Nice seeing you, Senator."

Fanny is oblivious to her mother's interest in wrapping up.

"Come on, there's time for one drink!" she says, all bright eyes and bushy tail. And then, seizing a moment she knows might not come again, Fanny says, "Senator, do you have room for an intern this summer? I would die to work for you! Really I would."

"Fanny! Please! The senator—"

"Would be very pleased to have an old friend's daughter on his staff," he says beaming at Fanny. "Just call me, Jen. Anytime. I'm sure we can set something up."

Barton Brock looks like he is going to explode.

Fanny, flushed, is still saying *Wow* and *Thank you* when her mother takes her arm.

"Goodbye, Lee," Jenny says, and hauls her daughter off towards the exit and into the warm, jasmine-scented San Francisco night.

"Senator. Work. Focus," says Barton Brock, all business, as he nods towards the waiting livery driver with the sign that says SEN. ROGERS & STAFF.

CHAPTER 4

"Mom! What the fuck was that about?"

Jenny is on a determined march to the parking lot and the car and from there to her Menlo Park kitchen where she looks forward to a good, relaxed dinner with her daughter.

"I don't know what you are talking about." Jenny wheels her Loft-issued rolling suitcase with fixed attention, eyes forward.

"Mom! The guy offers me a job and you give him the brush-off! What did he do? Make a pass at you or something?"

Jenny puts the key in the Jetta's ignition and starts the engine. Lee Rogers is not something Jenny wants to talk about with her daughter. Even with the daughter with whom she shares most everything.

"Yeah yeah, he's a letch, I saw it on *W.W.*," says Fanny, as if everyone in the world is as conversant as she is with Washington's cattiest gossip blog. "Everyone knows that about him. Wait, did you and he ever…?"

Jenny pilots the car out of the lot. "He was on a flight of mine, once, a long time ago. We had a nice chat."

"A 'nice chat'? Sorry, Mom, not buying. You ran away like he was a leper or something. What happened with you two? Fess up!"

"It was a long time ago." Jenny focuses on the highway.

"Whatever," says Fanny and shifts in her seat, crossing her arms. "We can leave it in the realm of unsolved mysteries if you like. But I'm taking him up on his offer."

"Absolutely not." Jenny isn't kidding around.

"What the actual fuck, Mom?" Fanny is genuinely confused.

And not happy to have a plum internship snatched out of her grasp.

Jenny fishes through the bins of her mind, trying to reel in a reason. "I don't want you living alone in Washington."

Couldn't be lamer. Fanny is, after all, living alone in New York in the fall when she starts up at Barnard.

Jenny lurches forth with unreason. "Yes. But that's in a dorm. With other girls."

"Hello? You live with other interns in Washington. Deborah Martin is going, I could room with her."

Jenny shifts gears. "Why would you want to be an intern anyway? A lot of coffee fetching. Xeroxing. Envelope licking. Really great experience."

Jenny accelerates. She's tired. She's tired of this conversation. She wants to have dinner with her daughter and not squabble over Lee Rogers.

"Look, Fanny, I just don't feel right about it. Please don't call him."

Fanny's a dog with a bone in her teeth. "We're talking about my future!" She is genuinely stumped by her mother's stubbornness and the more interesting question of what she doesn't want to talk about. "How often does an internship with a top-flight senator drop in your lap? C'mon, Mom! Tell me. What's with this guy? What'd you 'chat' about all those years ago, *Jen Jen*?"

Jenny is too tired to resist further.

"Okay. Okay. It was more than a chat. We had a few dinners."

"And?" She knows when "dinners" means more.

"And nothing. He's married. So I broke it off."

"Whatever. Twenty years later and he clearly wants to have a drink, 'to catch up.' So catch up, Mom. And while you're on the phone with him, put in a good word for your daughter. You know, the straight-A daughter. Make her happy."

Good idea, thinks Jenny. *Make your daughter happy. And change the subject while we're at it.* She takes a small box out of her bag. A nice, expensive looking box. Hands it to Fanny.

Fanny's face lights up. What's more fun than beautifully wrapped packages? Which, let's face it, are often far more exciting than what's inside.

"Déjà Vu!" says Fanny as she opens the box, takes out a crystal bottle, and turns it in her hand. Her eyes twinkle in the reflections cast. Déjà Vu, the par excellence of perfumes. Fanny's genuinely knocked out by her mother's generosity. "Mom," she says, "this cost a fortune."

"Nothing but the best for my daughter."

"Which is why," Fanny says, "I want you to talk to Rogers."

Jenny calls on her maternal authority: "Fanny. Drop. It."

The car speeds down Highway 101. Conversation skitters along in other directions. Fanny drops it.

But determination is written all over her face. There are lots of ways to skin the Washington internship cat. If her mom won't make the call, Fanny will find another way.

CHAPTER 5

Lee Rogers is very much on Jenny's mind as, at last, she lowers herself into a lavender bubble bath before bed. Not the Lee of earlier today but the Lee she met in…dear god, was it really the previous century?

"Your eyes look so blue in that shirt." It was a pretty dumb thing to say. (Why would anyone's eyes look more blue in a white dress shirt?) But the words tumbled straight out of Jenny's mouth when she met Lee Rogers on that flight from San Francisco to D.C. so many years ago.

Rogers lit up like a firework.

"Mostly sweet, a little bitter, that's how I like it," he said as Jenny placed a coffee cup on his seatfront tray.

Another charmer, Jenny thought. And his eyes *were* blue.

The Captain came on the speaker and let the passengers know they were passing over the San Juan Mountains and were more than thirty thousand miles above sea level and could expect a pleasant flight and were free to walk around the cabin. Rogers had Jenny's phone number long before the plane landed at Dulles.

Jenny remembers their exchange with pleasure—and some mild embarrassment—as purple bubbles gather on her chest.

"Nope," he told Jenny when she came to clear the dinner plates. "I'm not giving you the tray. Unless you give me your phone number."

"Sir, I need to clear your plate so that you can stow your tray table before landing. FAA Rules. Now tell me: why do you need my phone number?"

"I need your number because you are the prettiest girl in the sky." That's what Rogers had said. Jenny remembers listening intently when he added, "And I just left my kids in Colorado for a ski vacation, and I'm all alone, which is nice for now but in a day or so I'm going to be lonely and sad and a drink with someone just like you would cheer me enormously. Also, I'm a lot of fun, and I bet you'll have a good time."

Jenny remembers liking the odd mix of dopey lines and seeming straightforwardness. In truth, she doesn't know exactly what it was she liked about Lee Rogers or why she gave him her phone number but she did.

He called when he said he would, two days later. "Just as I thought," came the voice on Jenny's cell, "I'm lonely and sad, and a drink with someone like you would cheer me enormously." Arrangements were made.

The next day, after the 5PM flight from Atlanta landed at Dulles, she met Rogers for a drink. Two drinks in fact. After the second, Jenny was a little loopy. But not so loopy that she failed to take note of Lee Rogers' left hand, which did not have a wedding ring on it.

Rogers took Jenny's hand on the way out of the Capitol Bar. "Lets try Thai," he said. "Phuket." It wasn't so funny really but Jenny laughed a wild laugh and laugh succeeded laugh until dinner was done and Lee Rogers, leaning in, very politely said, "Come home with me." Easy as that.

The M Street townhouse was lovely and impressed Jenny, as did the fact, revealed in photos of children and horses and family holidays, that Lee Rogers was a very married man.

Jenny found herself a little intoxicated—not just by drink, but also by Lee Rogers, his attention, his charm, his hunger.

What happened in the guest bedroom of Lee Rogers' home had rarely happened either to Lee Rogers or to Jenny Cours. There was a blood-boiling madness to their connection. They could not have enough of one another. Afterwards both Jenny and Rogers enjoyed a singular sense of being both entirely sated and completely ravenous for more. It was a thrilling, exhausting night for both of them.

Jenny was up at 5:35 the next morning for an early-bird flight to Miami.

"Fly me to the moon. Or have dinner with me next Monday," Lee said into Jenny's cell about ten minutes after the plane landed in Florida. Jenny was charmed that he'd checked the arrival time and thoughtfully timed his call ten minutes after landing so that Jenny had time to clean the cabin and could devote her sole attention to him.

"Jupiter, Mars, say where you'll be and I'll be there," said Jenny. Monday was her day off. And she could fly Loft anywhere she liked.

Jenny sighs at the memory of how young she was. And how long ago it all seems now.

Intoxicated though she was by Lee and by a carnal adventure more intense than she'd ever dreamt she could have, Jenny Cours had enjoyed a happy life for too long to lose her head. She saw that she'd fallen hard for Lee in ways she couldn't control—she caught herself thinking about him when she should have been thinking about putting suitcases in overhead compartments. (She clopped two different passengers in the head with carry-on cases on the flight to San Francisco.) And she began to find it increasingly discomforting to sleep at night without him.

"Senator Rogers, I think I'm in love with you," she told Lee at dinner at one of their now twice-weekly D.C. trysts.

"You think?" said Lee with an odd blend of total surprise and complete awareness. (And yes, "Senator Rogers" was the pet name Jenny had used for Lee ever since she'd learned his occupation, on that first night at the Thai restaurant.)

"This is a problem for me, Senator. It's a problem because you are married—to someone else."

Rogers traded his teasing expression for one that was very solemn.

Jenny then said what every woman who has had the misfortune to fall for someone who is cheating someone else out of a husband eventually says: "This isn't right, Lee. I can't do this. I love you. But I can't."

A long silence followed. Then Rogers reached for Jenny's napkin. He wrote the following message, opening the napkin for extra room. "The part of me that is your friend and respects and admires you beyond measure wants you to have all this and more with someone who can make you happy, forever. The part of me that is in love with you wants never to let you go. In a nutshell, L." He handed the napkin to Jenny.

A woman less committed to her own best interest would have melted. Swallowed her resolve and gone with Rogers when he said, "Come on, let's go to the Ritz. We can have strawberries and champagne in bed and flip coins or throw darts or something that will help us out here."

Stretching her long legs out in the bath, Jenny smiles. A sad smile.

"No, Lee," she told him. "You'll never leave your wife. And probably you shouldn't. And I shouldn't go with you to the Ritz."

Jenny kissed the senator on the mouth, softly, hailed a cab for Dulles airport, flashed her Loft ID at the gate and got on the redeye flight west. She'd seen Lee Rogers once more after that, when she'd thought it might change everything; but it hadn't, and she hadn't seen him again, until this evening when she bumped into him at SFO.

CHAPTER 6

At another airport three time zones away, Nick Sculley saunters into the Hudson News at LaGuardia and picks up a pack of Skittles.

Nick Sculley is lanky, intense, preoccupied with…oh, who knows what preoccupies lanky, intense 32-year-old men?

His shirt is bright white and starched to within an inch of its life. Nick likes it like that, always has. This one is tucked into his jeans. Nick's Arthur Ashe shoes give him an athletic look. He could be a pro at one of the suburban country clubs nearby. Except he's not from the suburbs and country clubbing plays exactly no part in his life.

Nick fingers the stack of *New York Posts* at the newsstand register. *Goodbye to all this,* he thinks. Nick is heading west.

His photography career has not gone well in New York. No big tragedy or anything, but Nick hasn't quite panned out.

He had a promising start—in St. Louis at the *Post Dispatch,* where he had an Uncle, Mack, the night shift news editor, who gave him a new Leica camera and his first job, as an assistant on the news department's photo desk. That was in August of 2014.

A week later, a young white police officer called Darren Wilson shot an 18-year-old unarmed black man, Michael Brown, dead in the street in Ferguson, a nearby, mostly black town in the greater St. Louis area, in circumstances that would be the subject of heated debate and the occasion for what polite newspapers called "unrest."

The body of the dead black man lay in a sad and crumpled heap on the street for four full hours after the shooting and neither this nor the fact that the Ferguson police had a history of questionable incidents involving police violence against unarmed black men had contributed much to fellow feeling on the corner of Chambers Road and West Florissant Avenue when Nick arrived, with reporters, that evening.

Nick stepped forth into the big, noisy crowd just as police started lobbing tear gas at them.

He had just taken his camera out of the padded canvas case slung over his shoulder when a tall black man reached into the street and pitched a canister of smoking gas back at the police.

Snap. Snap. Snap!

Nick lucked into what turned out to be a series of good clean shots, one of which fast came to be the iconic image, the visual statement of race relations in the town of Ferguson, MO—and many other American cities during the summer of 2014.

It did not hurt that the black man who lobbed the tear gas canister back at the police happened to be wearing a shirt patterned with stars and stripes. Yes, an American flag shirt, which Nick had not even noticed when he took the shot.

Snap!

As it happened, the man was also holding in his left hand, as he reached for the canister with his right, a bag of potato chips emblazoned, in big red letters, with the words "The Flavor of America," which fact had also escaped Nick's attention at the time he took his shot.

Snap! Snap! Snap!

Millions of people saw Nick's image, which was tweeted 22,341,276 times and retweeted another 878,982 times in the week after Darren Wilson pulled the trigger on his police-issued gun.

It was on TV too, and on magazine covers and t-shirts sold not just in this country but also in Europe and elsewhere around the globe. Nick's phone started to ring and, a week after the shooting, he had a new agent, and also a ticket to the Big Apple. Snap!

Not quite. Nick had meetings with big-name editors at big-name venues and even sold a few pictures here and there. But the heat that Nick's iconic image generated evaporated far sooner than did the tension in the streets of Ferguson, which erupted once again, in November of 2014, when a St. Louis grand jury decided not to indict Officer Wilson in connection with the shooting.

Was it possible Nick had flamed out entirely just months after his career caught fire? It was an unsettling possibility. One that prompted Nick to redouble his efforts and spend the next year and change (ah, hell, call it what it was, two solid years) beating the bushes for work. None forthcoming, Nick found himself accepting an invitation from a college friend to travel out to L.A., regroup, maybe find work on a movie set.

He puts the Skittles in his brown leather messenger bag and makes his way down the concourse towards Gate 24, Flight 271, departing for Los Angeles, stopover in Vegas.

Nick is one of thousands of travelers in the concourse but it is Nick alone who has the great good fortune to pass the Admiral's Club Lounge just as its big mirrored door swings open and Elizabeth Diamond, nee Elizabeth deCarlo, formerly of Pennsylvania and more recently of Las Vegas, walks out.

The reinvented Elizabeth is a willowy blonde in a flowing skirt and high leather boots. She rolls a Louis Vuitton bag behind her as she heads towards the departure gates.

Nick does not notice the $3,200 bag. He focuses instead on Elizabeth. Her hips sway slightly in front of him as they walk towards the gates. He instinctively takes out his iPhone—the only camera he's got on him that isn't packed—and shoots.

Nick doesn't quite know why he's doing this, but some new muse is speaking to him. Suppose he photographed the beginning, the middle and the end of a relationship? Might that be the subject of a photo essay? Suppose they met, fell in love, married, had a slew of kids? It could be a whole book. But Nick is getting a little ahead of himself while his subject is getting away. He takes off after her.

And fate intervenes. She turns into Gate 24 and stops in front of him at the ticket counter. Maybe everything will be this easy from now on. Would be nice.

He shoots Elizabeth rummaging through her bag. "Where is that ticket?" she says to no one in particular and drops a slim paperback on the floor.

Nick pockets his iPhone and bends down and picks up the book (time to step out of the stands and onto the playing field). He sees that the book is Graham Greene's *The End of the Affair*.

"How strong is your faith?" Nick asks Elizabeth as he hands the book back to her.

"Excuse me?" She is still looking for the ticket in her bag.

"Would you give up the greatest love of your life for your faith?" Nick asks.

Elizabeth slows the excavation mission through her bag. "Oh the book. I don't know. I just started it. It's little. I needed something for the plane." She looks at Nick. She flashes him a heart-stopping smile.

Ever heard of lust at first sight? Nick has just discovered it.

"And you just spoiled the ending." Elizabeth looks Nick in the eye.

It will later become clear that Elizabeth Diamond is not much of a reader. Longing for a little distraction, she's been east on a weekend shopping trip with her friend Lisa who came up with Greene when Elizabeth asked if she had a book, a quick book, that she could finish on the five-hour trip home.

She fumbles for her ticket some more, finally turning it up. Then she looks up at Nick apologetically. "It's okay," she says, "even if you did spoil the ending. I'd much rather chat than read. I get so bored on these long flights to the coast."

Nick can't place Elizabeth's accent. Bedroom maybe.

Nick tells Elizabeth he'd love to join her. Yes, yes, yes, he definitely would like to join her. "But," he says glancing at her first-class boarding pass, "I'm traveling steerage."

"I'm sure we can do something about that," Elizabeth says. Then she smiles that smile again.

Nick watches her sway back to the ticket counter. There is something about her gait, or is it the golden hair, that puts him in mind of a lioness, and he is thinking pleasant thoughts of visiting her lair when she returns a few moments later with a new ticket in hand.

Fifteen minutes later, Nick sits snug in his economy-class seat. Elizabeth, gauzy skirt spread like a picnic blanket across her thighs, is beside him.

"Good seating arrangements. You're a bit of a miracle worker."

"It's not that hard to trade down to a tourist-class seat. That kid that was seated next to you is now in seventh heaven. He just ordered three dinners!"

Nick loves when her eyes brighten. He is not a practiced flirt. But it's coming very easily. Amazing what a little lust can do.

"Nothing like giving a leg up to the 99 percent," he says.

Elizabeth wants to know what percent Nick is. "Pure 99," he says. "But I have a plan."

"Really?" says Elizabeth. "Let's hear it. And make it slow. It's a long flight." She sinks into her seat.

Nick takes out his iPhone and snaps Elizabeth's picture.

"What's that for?" she asks.

Nick explains he's a photographer. And she inspires him.

"I'm probably not the first."

He smiles and knows it's time for a little colorful backstory.

He tells her he was the one who took the Ferguson photo that became *the* defining image of racial unrest in America.

"The guy with the flag shirt? The one who threw it back at the police?"

Nick tells Elizabeth yes, that's the one. (He doesn't mention that he hadn't noticed the man was wearing a flag shirt when he took the picture.)

Elizabeth looks disappointed. For one thing, she was looking for a longer tale. Maybe one that involved more planning and artistry, and less chance.

"Sort of like life, isn't it?" Nick says, trying to strike the right balance between self-confidence and self-deprecation. "Inadvertent fortune. You stumble into the right place at the right time. It would be better if you could say your actions were prompted by thought and not instinct, and much better if your good fortune led to more good fortune, a long and continuous series of happy endings, rather then a quick pop followed by a slow fizzle." He sounds every bit like the Brown Rhetoric Department grad he is.

Elizabeth gives him a small smile. "All *my* stories have long series of happy endings."

"Really?" says Nick, amazed by her audacity or whatever it is. "How do you manage that?"

"Ohhh," Elizabeth draws the word out, "stuff like seating myself next to you."

"And are we going to have a happy ending?"

Nick is amazed to find people—he, of all people—actually say stuff like this.

"Could be," says Elizabeth.

Let's hope, thinks Nick. *Happy Endings. Now there's a title for my photo book.*

The flight attendants make one of their endless announcements. Flight path. Altitude. Really? Who cares? But the heat of the moment dissipates and Nick and Elizabeth return to a quotidian conversation. Elizabeth wants to know why Nick is going to L.A.

The photo opened doors, but Nick explains that was a while ago. He kind of hit a wall in New York. So while he's waiting for the return of the muse or good fortune, he's decided to take his old college girlfriend's offer to bunk out on her couch in L.A. and see if he can get some movie work.

Hildy Akers recently starred in an indie hit and moved to Tinseltown to field the offers.

Elizabeth leans in close to him, tilts her head slightly to the side and gives Nick a long languorous kiss on the mouth.

She leans back in her chair. "Getting inspired?"

"Yes! Now I'm bursting with ideas," says Nick. Her smell— sugary, citrusy—knocks him out.

Elizabeth is pleased with herself. And she has an idea: "Why don't you come to Las Vegas? Forget the couch. My family has a cozy little apartment that's empty. And it has a bed! I'll get you a job on a local magazine. Come on. Take a wild chance."

"Is this one of those offers? The kind you can't refuse?"

"I wouldn't if I were you," says Elizabeth. She kisses Nick again, hard, then pulls back. And then she kisses him again, gently this time.

Nick tastes her lip gloss and thinks he can see stars.

God, she's good.

"Aren't you just a little bit curious?" Elizabeth is practically purring.

Yes. Nick is definitely curious. He's surprised to find himself entertaining practical thoughts. For example, he's thinking that he didn't check a bag through to L.A. so there's no reason at all not to get off in Las Vegas and, well, see what happens.

The flight attendant rolls up with a cart full of dinner trays.

"Chicken marsala or lasagna?" she asks.

"Yes," says Nick. "Yes, yes, yes." He looks over at Elizabeth and they collapse into giggles. The flight attendant looks at them like they are loopy or stoned or something, which they might as well be.

In truth, Elizabeth is not actually sure what she's doing. But it comes kind of naturally once she's in the swing of it. Toss a ball in the air. Does he bat it back? Yes! Toss another. Oh look! Right out of the park. Giggle. Smile. Kiss the boy. Watch him light up. Knowing how to speak to the animal in the man is half the game. The rest, Elizabeth finds, is really a matter of will. Does the woman want to go through with it or not? Knowing that this is really all that counts—at least with respect to the outcome of whatever conversation (yawn) is taking place on the surface—is a big part of Elizabeth's not insignificant power.

"I can't wait to get on the ground," Nick tells Elizabeth when, at last, they've sent the flight attendant on her way with her trays.

"To do what?" Elizabeth wants to know.

"To take off all your clothes." He says this like he means it. And he does. "I'm very good at undressing women."

Elizabeth explains that that will have to wait. Why? "Because I have to go home first. I'm a married woman."

"I see," Nick says.

"Does that bother you?"

"Should it?"

"I don't see why," Elizabeth says, "if it doesn't bother me."

And so begins a season of dreamy illicit afternoons in the Diamond-owned Desert Paradise apartment complex, where Nick makes himself at home as soon as Flight 271 from LaGuardia lands in Las Vegas in the dog days of summer.

CHAPTER 7

Nick's 12th-floor apartment is a mess. He doesn't pay attention to things like that.

Nick looks at his watch. It's nearly ten. He strides out of the apartment and into the elevator.

Nick checks himself out in the elevator mirror to make sure his starched white shirt is tucked into his jeans the way he likes. It is and he likes what he sees. So would most of the women in a thousand-mile radius.

The doors open. Nick walks into the lobby, crosses the garden-green carpet, sidles past a wall of bamboo (why bamboo in a Vegas apartment lobby? oh, don't ask) and walks to the delivery entrance door. You can never be too careful. Diamond's got eyes on his beautiful wife all over Las Vegas. Nick flips the latch so it can be opened from the outside, then steps away and watches in the mirror by the wall of mailboxes.

The door swings open just a minute later. Elizabeth Diamond, draped in a white chiffon dress, walks towards him, her red patent heels click-clicking across the floor as she does. Special delivery.

Her lips move up in a tiny flicker of a smile when she sees Nick; for one moment, her willowy white-blond hair sticks to her Wild Poppy lip gloss and smears, just a little.

Elizabeth wipes her lips, erasing both smear and smile. She returns to her expressionless expression. She does not look at Nick again. He walks ahead of her through the lobby and back to the elevator, where he enters "12" on the control panel. Elizabeth stands behind him. Studying her shoes.

The door opens. Nick gets in. Elizabeth gets in. The door closes.

Nick takes Elizabeth into his arms, slides his hand up her dress and squeezes her ass. Their kiss is deep, passionate, animal. It nearly knocks them out. When the doors open on 12, they stumble out dizzy and disoriented, the way people do when they get off roller coasters. Nick and Elizabeth go directly to the bedroom, tearing each other's clothes off on the way.

Afterwards Elizabeth stands naked next to the kitchen table drinking Fiji water from the bottle. Nick lies in bed watching her. He likes what he sees and picks up his iPhone and snaps a few pictures.

"More pictures?" Elizabeth purrs. "How do I look?"

"Fuckable," says Nick. He puts the phone down. He's got a way with words. But he's a little spent so you wouldn't necessarily know it now.

Elizabeth sets the bottle on the table, draws her initials in the dust on the fancy induction stovetop. "Don't you ever clean this place?" she says. (It's obvious he doesn't.) She opens the fridge looking for something to eat. She comes up with a peach yogurt.

(No, you wouldn't think a lanky, intense 32-year-old guy who is too busy with his intense 32-year-old life to bother cleaning his kitchen would eat peach yogurt. Don't understand people too quickly. Nick always says that.)

"Get one for me," says Nick.

"I'm not the help," says Elizabeth. God, she's good looking. "Besides, this is the last one. Someone needs to stock up."

Nick gets out of bed and pulls on his shorts. (Yellow and green with palm tree patterns.)

"This place is a disaster," says Elizabeth, looking into the empty refrigerator and the sink full of dishes next to it. "I remember when it was livable. Now it's a crash pad. Aren't you making enough money to hire a maid?"

"To do what?" Nick asks. "We only use the bed."

Elizabeth picks her clothes off the floor and starts to get dressed. "You're right," she says, slipping her dress over her head. "I've got to get used to dry cleaning my clothes after I come over."

Nick pulls her close and kisses her hard on the mouth.

"I love you, Nick—but do you know why all love stories end tragically?" Nick would like to know why. "Because the lovers can't get together. Ever."

"I wouldn't call this apart," Nick pulls Elizabeth very close.

"And I wouldn't call it happily ever after either," says Elizabeth.

"Happy today, aren't we?" says Nick.

"Gloriously." Elizabeth *is* glorious. In so many ways.

But she's also on a narrative tear. "Take Romeo and Juliet. Two kids from rival families that hate each other. The lovers face impossible obstacles. But they defy them and make secret plans, which of course, fail. And in the end, everyone dies for love. Great."

Nick looks absentmindedly at Elizabeth's thighs while she talks.

"We're not kids, Elizabeth," he says. He sits down at the kitchen table. In another world, one before cancer and surgeon generals, he would light a cigarette, probably Marlboro, and slowly inhale.

"No. We're older and wiser and just as fucked. I told you to get a girlfriend."

"But I don't want anyone else."

Elizabeth shakes her head. Neither does she. She kisses his mouth. She kisses his neck. Nuzzles his left ear. She's moving down his torso when she sees a half-packed bag on the floor. "Going somewhere?"

"You know you're not supposed to ask about my work. I'm going to find out about my new assignment today."

Elizabeth laughs. She's got a beautiful laugh—it's full of sunshine and something bright, wild poppies maybe.

"Don't dummy up on me, Capa," she tells Nick, "I got you the stupid job. Where are we going this time?"

Elizabeth puts her long leg in her high shoe as she repeats the question. Her grace takes Nick's breath away.

"Where are we going?" he says. "Nowhere. Here. We're going here. It's impossible to go anywhere else."

If he had one, Nick would definitely have another drag off his cigarette. "Do you think he suspects?" he says, not taking a drag of the cigarette he's not smoking.

"No," says Elizabeth, twisting her little foot into the high shoe.

"Why not?"

"Because if he knew I'd be dead."

And no, she's not being melodramatic. Elizabeth tells Nick there are rules for trophy wives. And Rule #1 is: no fucking around. And no, she can't leave either. Why? Because only he gets to call "game over."

"Suppose you break the rules?"

"There is a box. Six feet under. Waiting for me out in the desert."

"You've got to be kidding," says Nick. Elizabeth isn't kidding.

"Look, Nick, Bruce bailed me out when I was in a lot of trouble. I owe him, big time." She looks back down at the half-packed bag. "So what's the next junket? The next big scoop?"

"I don't know. He just told me to be ready to leave in twenty-four hours."

Nick puts his hand on her bee waist and pulls her towards him for another kiss. Or six or twelve. It's hard to tell where one ends and the next starts.

CHAPTER 8

Nick drives his '79 Cutlass Supreme into the *Vegas Today* parking lot. He has Maroon 5 on the radio as he zips the Olds into his reserved space, the one right next to Bruce Diamond's.

Diamond is a bit much. He's tall, handsome, and ridiculously rich. See the Ferrari in the *Reserved for the Boss* space? That's Bruce Diamond's car.

Diamond loves expensive cars, priceless paintings, beautiful women. He loves throwing huge piles of money around. He loathes losing anything and he has an ego as big as the MGM Grand. You know it the minute you see him. He's so full of himself and all of his big hungry qualities, he is near to bursting. It's actually fun to watch him in action. There aren't many people who are so completely as you see them.

Vegas Today, a super-glossy magazine, is distributed in every suite in Vegas. That includes the VIP, VVIP and VVVVVIP suites, the Safari Suite, Tahiti Suite, and every other suite and room in every hotel in Vegas, seven of which Diamond owns.

The magazine chronicles the lives of the high-toned desert dwellers. There aren't many of these. So it also devotes super-saturated high-end (expensive) ink to the entertainers, whales and rollers who pass through town. The magazine provides useful service pieces: the best microdermabrasion in the desert, the best four-handed massage, helicopter rides over the Grand Canyon.

Once, a long time ago, Bruce had journalistic aspirations. He likes to be in the thick of things, to have the story everyone wants to tell. He likes the idea of digging for dirt and coming up with gold. And pictures. Lots of them. Images you'll never forget. For a long time, he wanted to be that person. But his life took another turn and he wound up as a real estate speculator, a lucky one, so instead of being the guy who goes out and shoots the story, Bruce hired one.

At Elizabeth's nudging, the one he hired was the 32-year-old lost boy from St. Louis via New York who came West to shoot movie stars, stopped in Vegas and didn't leave.

Nick is the kid Bruce might have been. That's part of what bothers Bruce about Nick. The other thing that bothers Bruce about Nick is that Elizabeth, who met Nick on a flight from New York, tends to be a little giddy when she comes home from coffee dates with Nick and his starched white shirts.

Nick settles into his *Vegas Today* cubicle. Bruce sidles up before he even has a chance to hit the power button on the computer.

Bruce, all smiles, extends his hand and gives Nick his new assignment, the one he mentioned on the phone earlier. Nick listens carefully as Bruce sketches out the basics—a crazy murder, strange mind-boggling details, a Vegas connection (the perpetrator comes from a big-money casino-owning family)— and hands Nick an airplane ticket.

Nick's heart stops when he sees the destination stamped on the ticket: Wasilla, Alaska.

Wasilla fucking Alaska. Really? WTF? And how the fuck is he supposed to see Elizabeth when he's in some frozen boondock on a long-term assignment?

This, of course, may be a question Bruce had in mind when he dreamt up the assignment. The thought crosses Nick's mind when his cell vibrates in his pocket. He picks up the call.

"I need to see you, Nick. We fought. This morning. He hit me. This time I'm through."

Bruce is still standing right outside Nick's cubicle.

"Yeah. Okay. I see," says Nick. "What can I do for you?"

"Come here. I'm all packed up. Get me out of here."

Bruce looks at Nick. "Go ahead, buddy, take it. Call me from Wasilla," he says and walks away.

Nick stands up and walks outside where he can talk. There, in the parking lot, Nick ascertains that Elizabeth is keyed up but isn't hurt.

So he tells her, "You know that mystery assignment you asked about? It's a long piece. On a woman in Wasilla. Related to the Greens. She killed her six kids. They found them in a freezer under a frozen moose."

"Wasilla?" says Elizabeth, cooling down. "Isn't that Alaska?"

"Yeah. I told you, I'm sure he suspects us. He wants me out of town. Far out of town." The cars shimmer in the sun. Everything here is a mirage.

"Fuck him," Elizabeth says. "Come over here now."

"I can't, doll. Have to go to a staff meeting here. Can you hold on until the day ends? See you at 5:30?"

What can Elizabeth say?

The sun is still bright, dagger bright, when Nick pulls the blue Cutlass into Elizabeth's long circular driveway, the one that leads to Diamond's glass castle in the desert. Bruce opens the door.

"Come on in, homewrecker," he tells Nick. "Come to say your goodbyes? The missus will be down shortly. Meanwhile can I pour you a farewell drink?"

Though entirely unnerved, Nick plays it cool. Mostly because he has no idea what else to do. The house looks like a place James Bond would feel at home.

Bruce takes the bottle he is carrying and unscrews the top. He goes over to the bar to get some water and ice cubes and makes two Scotches on the rocks. He lifts his drink to Nick.

"Well, well, you surprised me. I didn't think you went in for this kind of cheesy stuff. Fucking the boss's wife. Pretty ballsy."

Nick finds it harder to play it cool. "At least I don't beat her."

Bruce laughs. Too hard. He follows this with an alligator grin. "How wrong you are." Now Bruce is overly cordial. "My dear backstabber! She does all the beating. I'm the one who suffers. It's suffering that drives me into the arms of other women. Very beautiful women, I might add."

Nick honestly has no idea where this is going.

"Mrs. Diamond is one selfish bitch," says Bruce. "She claimed she was frigid after I married her, and she's been ice cold ever since. Fucking her is like fucking a corpse."

"That's quite some discovery after you've been married all of, what, three months?"

"Tell me about it," Bruce says, and the edge in his voice could draw blood. "And you're the reason why, friend."

"Don't blame me if you can't keep your wife interested."

"You should know this about the woman before you take things any further. I don't think anyone or anything can keep that bitch interested. You know what I gave her for a wedding present? A Jean-Michel Basquiat. Cost me five million dollars. She took one look at it, shook her head, and shoved it in the back of her closet. Right behind her hundred fucking pairs of shoes. Can you imagine how much that hurt me?"

Elizabeth walks into the room in black jeans, white t-shirt, and a gorgeous coral necklace. Big Prada sunglasses cover her black eye. A purple blotch sneaks past the tortoiseshell frame.

"Speaking of my painting, where is it?" she says, as if she just happened into any old pool party chitchat. Nick is entirely weirded out. People talk like this? Really? *Maybe this wacko scene is something I can use somewhere*, he thinks. *In a book, in a script.*

The expression on their faces is priceless. What a time to leave his phone in the car.

"It's at the casino gallery, babe," says Bruce. "I didn't think it got an optimal viewing behind your shoe rack."

Elizabeth walks past Bruce and grabs Nick's hand. "Let's get out of here."

Now Bruce stiffens up. "Where are you going?" he says. "Your boy toy…"

Bruce turns to Nick. "You're fired," he says.

"…just lost his job," he continues.

Nick, unsurprised—this was hardly unexpected—is quick on the trigger. "Fuck you, Bruce, I quit. You can send someone else to Wasilla."

He pulls Elizabeth past Bruce, out the door, and into what is now the getaway car.

Elizabeth wants to know what Bruce said to Nick.

"He said you were frigid."

"Ha," says Elizabeth. "Do you know why he kept you around? Because he knew you got me hot and bothered. So when I came home from seeing you, he could screw me."

CHAPTER 9

Nick's Cutlass rolls past the palms on the desert highway. Elizabeth wants to know where he plans to go. "Away," says Nick.

Elizabeth puts her hand on his thigh. "Turn around," she says. "You have no money," she explains. "And no job. All I've got is in that little suitcase." She nods her head to the pink RIMOWA bag in the back. "And there's nothing in there we can eat. Go to the Majestic, will you, Nick?"

The Majestic is pretty much the most over-the-top hotel in Vegas. Which is saying a lot. It's a little Roman Empire replete with meticulous recreations of the Spanish Steps, the Trevi Fountain and the Coliseum. The elevator men wear gladiator costumes.

Diamond spared no expense here. No detail is too absurd. Ornate frescoes—in 24-karat frames—dot the ceiling. Diamond's personal art collection lines the walls and fills the galleries off the Parthenon-themed lobby.

Nick pulls his Cutlass into Valet Parking. (The valets wear togas.) Elizabeth tells Nick to stay in the car.

"Wait a minute, babe. They're not just going to hand over your painting," he says. She is already halfway out of the car. Elizabeth explains that Mike Masters, Bruce's head of security, is her buddy and would do anything for her. Plus, he happens to hate Bruce. The shiner ought to clinch things.

"Don't you think Bruce alerted these guys? Even if Mike's on your side, he's just one guy. No way they're going to let you waltz out with a five-million-dollar painting."

"Just give me five minutes. You'll see." Elizabeth flashes her killer smile. It's the smile that's driven him mad since he first saw it on the plane to Vegas. But smiles only take you so far. Nick wants to mess around with Elizabeth, in bed. He does not want to mess around with multi-million-dollar paintings or rich guys who punch their wives.

"Forget it, babe. I'll get another job. I'll finish my photo book and sell it for a bundle. We'll manage."

"Like a dream. Those coffee table picture books really sell." Elizabeth tips her tortoiseshell glasses down her nose and gives Nick a *Yeah, right* look and gets the rest of the way out of the car.

She takes Nick's face in her neatly manicured hands and gives him a long luscious kiss.

"You. Are. The. Best." Her lips are still moist from the kiss. "Take another picture of me for your book."

Nick slides his iPhone out of his pocket and snaps a picture of Elizabeth throwing him one more kiss. "Make sure you use all the naughty ones, and send a copy to Bruce!"

"Don't even joke about it," Nick says.

"Don't forget me," she calls as she heads towards the lobby door. "Back in five."

Elizabeth is not back in five. After twenty minutes Nick is an uncomfortable combination of bored, anxious and hot. He gives Elizabeth another five minutes. Then he parks the car and goes inside the casino. He looks around the lobby, sees Romulus and Remus but no sign of Elizabeth.

A security guard—please don't ask what he's wearing—points the way to Mike Masters' office.

No, Mike hasn't seen Elizabeth Diamond. No, she hasn't been in the lobby. No, she hasn't asked for anything. Anything else he can do for Nick? No, no, no.

There's a picture of Cleopatra on the ladies room door. Nick opens it up and yells Elizabeth's name. At the sink, a woman dabs mascara onto her lashes. "Hey! This is the ladies room! Get out!" She's annoyed and non-responsive when he asks if she's seen a tall blonde in black jeans. No, she says when he repeats the question, she hasn't.

Nick wanders down the hall, turns in at the Diamond gallery by the lobby. A group of high school kids stands in front of a painting—Elizabeth's Basquiat!—but there's no sign, there or elsewhere, of Bruce Diamond's fifth wife.

Hours later Nick lies on the hood of his car staring, blankly, at the Majestic entrance.

"Why. Why. Why did I ever let her go in there?" he asks himself helplessly, truly at a loss for what to do next. Why aren't we home in bed, and where is she? His questions are fruitless. Where the fuck is she?

CHAPTER 10

A mahogany box, top-of-the-line casket, lies in fresh-dug earth. Elizabeth, stretched out inside, desperately pounds on the lid, screaming for help.

But there is nothing nearby other than a vast expanse of Nevada desert.

Nick's blood pumps fast, throbs hard against his heart wall.

He awakens to the feel of a woman's arm on his shoulder. "Are you all right? Looks like you had a very bad dream."

Nick opens his eyes and sees Marsha, his agent's assistant, leaning forward and looking at him with real concern.

"Mmm. I'm okay, Marsha. Thanks. I must have dozed off. Wow. Bad dream. Yes. Really bad," he tells her. "Will it be much longer?" Marsha tells him no, Manny is ready, Nick can go right in.

Nick pulls himself together and walks into Manny's office. That might be too dignified a name for the dim room with the tiny window where his 57-year-old agent sits at a rickety desk full of manuscripts and papers. By the look on Manny's face, Nick can see his book proposal was a bust.

Nick starts selling. Hard. But Manny isn't buying.

"It could be bigger than Mapplethorpe," says Nick.

"That's great," says Manny, "I wish I was his agent."

"What didn't you like about it?" Nick asks.

Manny opens Nick's portfolio and starts thumbing through the pictures.

"That girl is hot, especially with her clothes off, but it's called *Happy Endings* and there isn't one. Happy or otherwise. It's just a bunch of girlfriend snapshots. What's the story? I met her on a plane, screwed her countless times, and she waved goodbye?"

"What's supposed to happen?" Nick says. "Let's see, a couple kissing goodbye? No, wait. They kiss and float off on a raft, into a sunset. Is that what you want?"

"I want you to get a paying job. There's no book here. How's your French?"

Nick says his French is okay, thanks. Why?

"A friend of yours. Hildy Akers. She's doing a picture in Paris. She made a special request for your services."

Hildy in Paris? Last Nick remembered, she'd moved to LA. But that was a few months ago now. Just because Nick's career is stalled doesn't mean everyone's is.

"I'd be doing what?" he asks.

Set photographer. Miss Akers is starring in a remake of *Vertigo*.

"What a great idea, remake one of the most revered pictures in cinema history."

"The story was originally French," Manny explains. "And they didn't like the American version."

"Who's 'they'?"

"Bernard Pascal."

"Never heard of him."

"I'm sure he's never heard of you either."

Nick looks down at his shoes, shaking his head.

Manny wants to know if Nick has anything better to do and asks, "Would a couple of prepaid months in Paris kill you? Steel yourself, Nick. It's a job."

Nick looks defeated. "It's not photography, Manny."

"You want to know what they're paying for *not photography*?"

Nick is on the next flight to Paris.

What's that old saying? A payday is a terrible thing to waste? Something like that. Nick figures he can work on *Happy Endings* in his spare time. You know, in between croissants and café au laits.

CHAPTER 11

Haines Johnson wears a red tie. A power tie. But Haines does not need a tie to convey his power. It is evident from his posture that he is at home in the world of dealmakers, power brokers, Sunday golfers.

There aren't many African American men (in fact, other than Johnson, there aren't any) dressed in expensively tailored Italian suits and John Lobb shoes in the banquet room at the Lackawanna Station Hotel in downtown Scranton.

Johnson would command attention even if he weren't standing at a podium, in front of a shimmering gold curtain, under a crimson "RE-ELECT LEE ROGERS" sign, in a room full of well-heeled potential campaign donors.

Tables full of "high net worth individuals" fiddle with rubber chicken while Johnson winds up his introductory remarks.

"Ladies and Gentleman, I'm honored to welcome the 2016 Parent of the Year, Senator Lee Rogers!"

Johnson joins the applause that Rogers excites as he (and his high-voltage smile and expensive haircut) move towards the podium.

Older and wiser than he was during his first campaign for Senate, Rogers has the same general regard for applause. He treats it the way porpoises regard the shiny red balls they balance on their noses. He chases it. He relishes it. He plays it for all it's worth. Applause is his favorite toy.

"Please, please," he tells the crowd, all smiles and twinkling eyes.

Rogers waves his hands downward. Please, please, he signals

the crowd, quiets the applause. "Shh shh shh" issues from the expensive dentistry and high-watt brightness that is his smiling mouth.

"The first thing I want to tell you about political life is that when a candidate does this—" Rogers waves his hands downward again. "What they really mean is this!" The senator waves his hands up, up, up.

Rogers elicits laughter, more applause. The ball is back on his nose.

Enough fun! Rogers puts down the ball and clears his throat and gets ready to launch into what is both a routine and also a rousing stump speech. But first a few introductory remarks of his own.

"It is a great pleasure to be here today with all of you. This is an extraordinary organization. Kudos and applause for all of you. Thank you for the generosity—and good sense—that motivated your decision to donate the proceeds from this event to Save The Children, a wonderful charity.

"Now, before I go on, let me say a word about this Best Parent award. I think you have made a mistake. I hate to admit it but I am not the best parent of the year."

"Oh no—" A collective groan sails from the crowd on the banquet floor.

Rogers has the red ball on his nose again. He continues: "But I'm happy to say the best parent of the year *is* here with me today, and that is my wife, right down here in front, Connie Rogers."

The claque of suits seated at Connie's table rise and applaud. She is lovely, a woman who exudes an evanescent, immediately likable quality. Warmth. Authenticity. It's hard to say exactly what it is but you get the feeling it would be as easy—and as rewarding—to swap recipes with Connie as it would be to talk about the latest Alice Munro novel or the Matisse exhibit at the Philadelphia Museum.

Connie looks a little older than her husband but she has a great smile. It's easy to see why the audience responds when she stands up and blows her husband a kiss, turns and waves to the cheering crowd, and basks in their affection.

Connie radiates so much warmth that it isn't immediately obvious how very thin she is. You can tell when she bends down into her seat. (And Mrs. Hines, who is seated beside her, notices that Connie's hands tremble in the sleeves of her navy blue bouclé dress before she folds them tightly together on her lap.)

Rogers gives his wife an affectionate wink, clears his throat again (what is that politicians always have in their throats, anyway?) and retakes claim of the audience.

"By the way, Haines, I was happy to hear you have a modern marriage in which everything is negotiable," says Rogers. He turns obligingly towards the man who introduced him and sits now at the center table. "I need some advice on that deal. I don't get much slack at home."

Connie casts her husband an adoring glance. She's tickled— and proud—that her husband is sharing a bit of their private language with a big audience, one she badly hopes will re-elect Lee to the Senate.

Fanny Cours stands at the back of the room, squinting through a viewfinder. The camcorder in her hand is trained on Senator Rogers. "Slack at home?" she says to herself. "Bad vibes."

CHAPTER 12

Fanny Cours, fresh from Barnard's orientation week, sips beer at the Railroad Car Bar at the Lackawanna Station Hotel.

"Wish me luck," she tells Hart McCoy, her mop-topped, moon-faced, twenty-year-old fellow videographer from Columbia.

Is there an evolutionary reason boys of a certain age look so much geekier than girls? Fanny, clad in a small black skirt, dark tights and army boots, looks like she lives on a planet near, but alien to, the one where young McCoy lives.

"Go get him, Fan," says McCoy. He sips his beer. He could use a hairbrush.

"I'm telling you," she says, "he really needs me, Hart." Her charm isn't entirely lost on Hart. But he doesn't register its full measure.

"And you need him, or you're going to have sprung for these train tickets for nothing," says McCoy. Beer foams up in the corner of his mouth.

Fanny gives McCoy a fist bump and strides through the swinging Railroad Car Bar doors into the Lackawanna. She sees Senator Rogers there, on a plump red velvet sofa, having a drink with his campaign manager, Barton Brock.

Fanny walks straight towards them. She stops directly in front of them with Hart's camcorder in hand and waits. The men keep talking, and then finally look up with practiced *what-can-we-do-for-you-young-lady?* expressions.

"Senator Rogers?" says Fanny. She sounds a little like a kid who's interrupted the captains of a particularly complicated dodgeball game on the neighborhood playground.

"Yes?" says Rogers. He's used to this.

"Remember me?" asks Fanny. A vague hint of something awkward passes over her features.

The senator gives Fanny a perplexed, thoughtful smile. Then his face goes blank and it looks like he's trying to find something in a dark closet. "I'm sorry," he says, "I know we've met, but can't recall just where it was."

The senator has opened the door. Fanny jumps right through.

"Yes. Yes. Yes!" she says. "At the San Francisco airport. With my mom. Jenny Cours."

Bingo! Rogers' face lights up. Of course. Jenny's daughter.

"What can I do for you, uh—"

"I'm Fanny. Fanny Cours. I'm a videographer. And you need me. You really do."

The senator is slightly taken aback by Fanny's directness. Which he vaguely remembers from the airport meeting. But he is not uninterested. People approach him all the time. But he can't remember a time anyone told him how much he needed them.

"I do?" he says. "Is that so?" *Go on*, he seems to add, but does not say aloud. *Tell me more. Play me.*

"Yes. You do. You really do." Fanny stares directly into the senator's eyes. "You need to show the voters who you really are. Without filters. Or spin doctors. Just the true Lee Rogers." Fanny holds up the camcorder. "And this can do it. I can do it."

Rogers isn't sure what she's selling but he genuinely wants to know more.

"I'd like to be your campaign's videographer. I can shoot you behind the scenes, off the stump, when you're talking seriously to friends." Fanny nods to Barton Brock. "About the future of America and why it matters to voters—and why Senator Lee Rogers' re-election ought to matter too."

Now that he's pushing fifty, Brock's tall, muscular build carries the extra weight that comes with campaign trails and months of rubber chicken. But the basic outline of a former running back is still visible under his navy blazer. When he stands, he looms. He has zero interest in hearing more about Fanny or her "videography."

(Fanny lost Brock's interest with the words "without filters." For Brock *is* the chief filter for Senator Rogers.)

"I'm sorry," he says, sounding about as sorry as a klansman at a lynching, "but we were just talking about where we might go around here to find a decent meal. Look, Miss—" Paying Fanny the pettiest dis imaginable, Brock makes a point of showing he's already forgotten her name.

"It's Cours," she says, "Fanny Cours. Videographer."

"Okay, Miss Coarse, I'm afraid the senator is very busy. Thanks very much for your interest. And good luck to you."

Rogers crunches a cocktail peanut in his teeth, chases it with a sip from his glass and tells Brock to hold off and let the lady have her say.

Brock is impatient. "Look, Lee, our media people are not going to—"

Fanny beats him to the end of the sentence. "What?" she says. "Your media people are not going to like the real Lee Rogers?"

Brock wonders if he should push Fanny aside, take the senator's arm, and just head out for dinner. Or should he leave Fanny enough rope and let her hang herself?

Fanny plows ahead. "Are you happy with the image you've got?" she asks Rogers. "The candidate who says he represents working men and women and then goes out and gets a five hundred dollar haircut? Are you happy with people seeing that Lee Rogers?"

Somehow Brock gets roped into debate. "Look, lady, that

was an unfortunate—isolated—incident. A video the opposition research people leaked to the press. That's it." He leaves out the fact that he was himself the opposition research person who'd leaked it.

"Right," says Fanny, "and you need my video to answer that video—and others that may come. Video I can shoot. Video that can be on Facebook instantly. I know how to do it, last summer I worked with PETA."

"People for the Ethical—?" Brock is mocking as much as he is asking.

"Treatment of Animals, that's right. I shot video that documented animal abuse, got it on Facebook, and it led to two slaughterhouses closing down. They said that themselves, that it was because of PETA's video. *My* video. Now I look at what the media is doing to Senator Rogers and it sickens me. It's so unfair. He's devoted his life to supporting American workers and those Tea Party nuts make him look like a slick ambulance-chasing shyster who spends all day posturing to get votes and then goes home to his thirty-thousand-square-foot mansion. My videos can correct that image."

Brock is more interested than he'd like to be. "Really," he says, "and how are you going to do that?"

Fanny stares deep into Rogers' eyes.

"Just by talking with him openly and honestly." Fanny keeps her eyes on the senator. "Asking him questions, letting him respond. That's all. And this lens," she taps the camera, "this mirror of the soul, will reveal Senator Rogers and his true character, the one that lives and breathes beyond the spin, beyond opposition research and all the rest."

Rogers has an odd and unexpected feeling of self-consciousness. It's uncomfortable, in an interesting way. Self-doubt is exciting new terrain for him. Fanny doesn't take her eyes off of him as she extols his integrity.

"Well," he stutters, slightly off his game, "I'm hardly a saint."

Fanny quickens to the feel of genuine, palpable interest she's aroused. A surge of confidence follows.

"Close enough," she says. She sways back from the senator. "Please. Let me show the world what I see."

CHAPTER 13

Elizabeth wants to disappear. From Bruce, from Nick, from the endless days of shopping and yoga classes, from all of it.

And now she can. Mike was a prince about the painting. Yanked it right off the wall and replaced it with the reproduction the gallery had used during the interregnum when the original was living in her shoe closet.

Who would know the difference? Not the slot machine players wandering through the gallery at 2AM, who can barely see straight after hours of spinning cherries and lemons.

Mike's whole body implied *Routine touch-up is all* as he marched out of the gallery with the Basquiat tucked under his arm and loaded the canvas into Elizabeth's rented SUV. She knew a dealer she could offload it to for cash, even if only a fraction of what it was worth. And then?

Goodbye Basquiat, goodbye Lost Fucking Vegas, goodbye Bruce Diamond jerk-off money-mad control-freak prick, goodbye Nick Sculley head-in-the-clouds wannabe photographer. Good fucking bye to all of you.

Turns out Elizabeth Diamond was more sick of the sorry state of her life as a blonde playtoy than even she knew.

Yeah, yeah, there were things about Nick that Elizabeth would miss: his long arms, his lean form, the muscled mass in the back of his thighs which had an animal power Elizabeth liked.

But she could and would do nicely without the dirty apartment and low-rent ambitions. "The pictures, the pictures, I'm going to make a best-selling book, cash in and take you away from all this."

Yawn. How many times did Nick say this? It tired Elizabeth to remember.

And, of course, Nick only had to say it once in order to make clear what a wobbly grasp on reality he had. To be charged up with great artistic ambition at a time like this! And in a place like Vegas.

All that gobbledygook she told Nick across a pillow? She meant some of it. But now she can't even remember what it was she said. And she has other things on her mind anyway.

Elizabeth is thinking that Bruce will probably spend a fortune on private detectives trying to run her, Nick and the painting down. Unless she does something to make him think there's no point. Which is why she leaves the SUV a smoking wreck on the side of the highway, a stretched canvas (courtesy of the dealer she sold the Basquiat to) burned to cinders in the back seat. With luck, that'll take care of Bruce going after her and the painting.

She hopes Bruce doesn't badger Nick too much. *The kid's probably tearing himself up over my disappearing like that.* But so what. Sometimes you fuck, sometimes you're fucked. That's how it goes.

One of the men Elizabeth knew in Vegas (in a special, every-other-Monday kind of way) told her that a good body is like money in the bank. Now Elizabeth has cashed out.

Two days later, after ditching the painting and depositing the money, Elizabeth is on a Trailways Bus, headed east towards… actually she's not sure exactly where and she doesn't care much either. Like Nick said, she's just headed away.

Neither Nick nor Bruce nor the guy in the Diamond Hotel on Monday afternoons, nor any of the other guys Elizabeth has known in Vegas or Pennsylvania, would recognize her. She doesn't look at all like the old Elizabeth—any of the old Elizabeths. Her blonde hair is black now, and it's short in a dykey kind of cut. She's dressed in such bad taste she hardly recognizes herself: jeans, turtleneck sweater, cheap, barely leather bomber jacket.

New skin, baby.

She's still a hot ticket and she knows it. Which probably increases her temperature at least another ten degrees. She has a wild, ready-for-anything feeling she hasn't had since she was 16.

CHAPTER 14

Fanny sits across from Rogers. He's at the desk, outfitted as all hotel rooms now are with an iPad charging station, stationery no one will ever use and a list of hotel services bound in a leather cover.

Fanny, on a fluffy upholstered chair with palm tree fabric, holds the camcorder in front of her, looks through the viewfinder and zooms in on Rogers.

Her authority is tenuous. She looks like she's filming scenes of a toddler's birthday party.

"It must be very difficult for you to campaign while your wife suffers with Parkinson's," Fanny prompts Rogers in an unthreatening, vaguely singsong voice.

Rogers responds with the same self-seriousness he deploys in interviews with policy experts or Senate colleagues.

"It's okay," he says. "And what I'm going through is nothing compared to Connie. The drugs she takes just exhaust her. But she is determined we fight this out."

"How does that make you feel?" Fanny puts a comforting hand on the senator's arm.

Rogers regards Fanny with great gentleness. "Sometimes," he says, "it is too much. The uncertainty. Connie could be paralyzed, completely, in ten years. Or in a year. We just don't know. Her one wish is for me to get re-elected. And I'm doing everything in my power to make that happen for her. It has nothing to do with personal ambition. I just don't want to disappoint her."

Is Rogers for real? His eyes well with tears. He wipes them away. Then he regains composure.

"Enough of me tonight," he says. "Let's get some sleep. The plane waits for no one tomorrow."

Fanny trots across the street to her motel room. The campaign is exhausting, but cool. The access is heady. There are other young people on the campaign team but no one has as much up-close-and-personal contact with the senator as she does.

On the morning flight, Fanny sits right across the aisle from Rogers. Even if she weren't pointing a camera at the senator and commanding a fair share of his attention, Fanny would be the correct answer if someone asked "Which thing on this plane is not like all the others?"

Most of the senator's staff is male. Young brash policy wonks and fast-talking wannabe back-room boys. Most are at least a little older than Fanny.

She's wearing a cute Agnès B cabbage rose print blouse, smart black skirt and short black boots. And holding a camcorder.

Brock is sitting next to the senator in seat 1B. The croissants on the campaign jet aren't French bakery quality or anything but they're not bad. Rogers has a nibble and turns to Brock.

"I've come to the conclusion that I actually want the people in Pennsylvania, the voters, to see who I am, who I really am. I don't know what the result will be. But, for me personally, I'd rather succeed or fail based on who I really am."

He has the same earnest look he had the previous day when he teared up talking about Connie and her determination. "Not some plastic Ken doll that you put up in front of audiences. That's not me."

And so begins Fanny's series of webisodes. In short order Fanny tapes, collects and catalogs more than a dozen video clips. These are posted on the senator's Facebook page, with short, matter-of-fact titles: *3:55PM: Arrive at Town Hall, Pittsburgh*;

6:30PM: Wheels Up, En Route, Allentown; 8:30PM: Law and Order Society Reception, Philadelphia.

Day Two of videography sees the senator and his entourage boarding another campaign plane. Rogers has a seat next to Michael Weldman, his speechwriter. They've got important work to do. But Rogers' mind is not on the finishing touch he's supposed to put on the speech he'll deliver shortly after the plane lands in Harrisburg. He pays Weldman little attention, and instead grins at Fanny and the camera she has trained on him.

"If any of these guys aren't nice to you, you just let me know."

Ha ha ha. Laughs issue forth from the seats around the senator. But not from Barton Brock, who barely manages a tight smile. He's focused on business, been around the bend with duplicitous sirens before, and neither Fanny nor her flowery blouse make any difference to him.

Rogers holds a yellow legal pad up to Fanny's camera.

"I just finished my foreign policy speech. It's sure to ruffle a few feathers. Can you read it?"

"Yes, I can read it," says Fanny moving the camera from Senator Rogers' smile to the yellow pad in his hand. " 'Into.' Into?" she says, trying to comprehend.

"No, it says 'Intro,'" Rogers explains. "I don't know what that's going to be yet. I'll make it up when we get there."

Into. Intro. Fanny is embarrassed to have confused the two. She makes a mental note to focus a little more carefully.

Inside the Pennsylvania State Education Association, she stands just to the left of the podium where Rogers will deliver his foreign policy speech. Five minutes before showtime, he pulls a Mont Blanc fountain pen from his jacket pocket and scratches a few final thoughts on his legal pad.

He's up and running a few moments later.

"Enough," he says. "Our time has come. Let's focus on building our own infrastructure, our own economy, our own education resources. Let's end our policy of intervention, occupation and nation building on far shores. Instead let us strengthen America's values, America's resources, America's future. Ladies and gentlemen, there is work to be done. Real work. Right here at home, in the land we love."

The nuances of the start of Rogers' speech may have been lost on Fanny and perhaps the rest of the assembled State Education Association members in the room. But the applause is no less thunderous for that. It's red ball time again! Rogers and team are satisfied with their efforts and revel in their reception.

Back on board the campaign plane that evening, Rogers takes a quiet moment out to consider his success. He is distracted, however, by Michael Weldman's shoes. And the sudden memory that Fanny's camera is, as it has now been for days, probably rolling.

Rogers barely misses a beat. He looks up at Fanny and her camera and says in a *cool-as-a-cucumber, of-course-you're-there-watching-me* kind of way, "Are those shoes cool? I have no idea what's cool."

Rogers smiles at the lens. Will Fanny help set him straight? What is cool? What shoes does she like? Then he's back on his senatorial track.

"Do you think most people have any idea what we are doing when we're off stage? I mean, really, 24/7 we're programmed to stay on message, to say what's safe and political," Rogers continues. "It's hard to shed all that. I think it helps to have you filming all the time—like now when I'm thinking, like real people do, about things like shoes—instead of just when I'm standing in front of a crowd. I absolutely believe this videotaping has the potential to change how we campaign, in a very good way. I mean it's like having the eyes of T.J. Eckleburg upon you all the time."

Fanny gets the reference to *The Great Gatsby*, which she read in her eleventh-grade English class, and is temporarily distracted. But she is intent on not losing focus.

So much so that she doesn't think to respond when the senator says, "Are those shoes cool, Fanny? What do you think?"

The camera is rolling again later that evening, after the senator's staff dinner. Rogers retires to his room in the Radisson Hotel. (Why are hotel drapes always made out of heavier cloth than drapes anywhere else? It definitely adds to the cocoon-like feel of the generic hotel room and contributes to the idea that a hotel is a separate universe, entire unto itself.)

Relieved not to have to concentrate on policy issues, Fanny returns to issues closer to the senator's emotional bone.

"You've had a lot of experience with suffering. You've spent much of your life as a lawyer representing people who have suffered as a result of corporate irresponsibility or oversights. What has this taught you?"

The senator shows no sign of the exhaustion that might slow a lesser man who spent an entire day racing around the state, pumping hands, exchanging views, making promises, refining promises, pumping more hands.

"All the pain I've witnessed has been part of my own personal faith journey. Because I've done what I think a lot of Americans have done, which is…I was raised in a very Christian home. But when I went to college, I drifted from my faith. Even after my brother, sister and mother died in a car accident, I drifted. After Connie and I got married, I drifted still. We went to church, of course, but I did not have the kind of day-to-day living faith I have today. But in 2000, on a day I will never forget, when Connie was diagnosed, my faith came roaring back."

Fanny switches off the camcorder. She is moved. Rogers is moved. They stare blankly at one another, tears in their eyes. Fanny makes a barely audible, but affecting, gulping noise.

"I'm so sorry," she tells Rogers, "I'm so unprofessional! It's just that…all that death. And illness. Overwhelming. So much loss…"

Rogers reaches for her forehead. "Fanny," he says, "you're burning up. Take that jacket off."

Fanny stands up and unzips her leather jacket and lays it on the chair, on top of the camcorder.

Rogers takes Fanny's hand, steadies her, leads her over to the bed and sits her down.

"I'm so sorry. I'm so sorry," Fanny says.

"Stop apologizing. You're working too hard." Rogers sounds sincere.

"I so want my videos to be good. To show everyone what a truly good man you are." Fanny straightens herself up on the bed.

Rogers is sheer reassurance. "They've been great. I hear we're getting a lot more traffic on my Facebook page."

"Really?"

"Absolutely." Rogers is happy to supply whatever medicine Fanny requires. "Yes, yes. Let me tell you, they've won over a lot of skeptics."

"Not Brock," says Fanny.

"He's old school. He'll come around."

"He doesn't like me very much."

"No. No. He's just overprotective."

"I'm just doing my job," says Fanny. Again, that endearing earnestness.

"I know that," says Rogers. "And I'm really the only one whose opinion matters."

"You *are* such a good man," says Fanny. She lays her head on Rogers' shoulder.

"Miss Cours. Miss Cours. What am I going to do with you?"
The conversation is taking a new direction.

"As my grandmother would say," Fanny offers, "the proof is in the pudding." They both laugh. Fanny looks into the senator's eyes.

"Why are you so good to me?" The words slip out of Fanny's mouth. She isn't thinking about what she's saying. Everything is so natural, easy.

Rogers is having an easy time too. "Because I believe in you, Fanny, and I believe in what you're doing. What we're doing."

"What are we doing?"

Rogers pulls Fanny into his arms and kisses her hard on the mouth. They fall back onto the bed in a tangle of limbs.

The senator pulls away, but just for a moment. He holds Fanny's face in his hands. Then, beginning with her nose and moving then to her eyes—first the left, then the right—and back to the corner of her mouth, he covers her with kisses.

Have you ever looked at someone and thought: *Take me, nothing on earth matters but that you kiss me hard and have me whole and crush me with your body?* This is what Fanny is thinking.

Rogers thinks, *How can I get her clothes off?*

The senator slides his hand between Fanny's legs. He feels her heat. He's looking for a go-ahead. And it looks like he has it. *Bravo!* he thinks.

Fanny thinks, *Lee Rogers, you are the love of my life.*

Lee Rogers unbuttons Fanny Cours' blouse. He looks into her eyes to see how emphatically they are saying "Yes." Satisfied with what he sees, he slips his thumb behind the band of her Le Mystère bralette which, in one quick move (a practiced slide of thumb and forefinger), he removes. The senator takes in the young girl and her fetching half nakedness.

Fanny thinks, *Take me Lee Rogers, I love you.*

Rogers positions Fanny back on the bed and begins to explore her body, her neck, her breasts, the soft skin behind her neck, with his mouth. He does not stop until he hears Fanny start to moan, softly, hungrily. Rogers likes this sound and is pleased with his effort.

For Fanny this is at least twelve worlds apart from the few experiences she had in high school. Those were clumsy and goal directed. This is something different entirely.

The senator unbuttons his shirt, drops it to the floor, and presses his naked chest against Fanny's. Fanny will try hard to remember the sequence of what follows but won't be able to, as it all happens in the fevered heat of a desire she has never known or even imagined.

Rogers parts Fanny's legs with his knee. He pulls her tights down and off. Now she is naked before him. He takes a moment and looks up, at Fanny's face, before he lowers his head and has a taste of her sex.

Fanny wriggles free. She wants to look Rogers in the eye. She wants to see him, touch him, smell him, drink him in. She wants to feel his mouth on hers. She wants—

Rogers turns her around, pulls her back against the edge of the bed, lifts her rear slightly into the air, and then, unable and really not so interested in waiting any longer, he plunges into the soft ready videographer and her choice little pussy.

Rogers is lost in his own rhythm. He has one hand on Fanny's breast (firm, peach shape) and uses the other to pull her back against him as he moves deeper inside her.

"Kiss me," says Fanny softly. Rogers tries to put his mouth on the back of her neck. But he's distracted and can't get his mouth in the right place. Or hear the breathy words Fanny is saying. The senator's body is far ahead of him now, deep, deep, deep, and he cannot and doesn't want to stop. Fanny is saying something like "Oh!" "God!" "Lee!" when he comes hard inside her.

"That was intense," says Rogers when it's all over. He looks at Fanny spread out before him and thinks, *What a tasty lunch.*

And then he rolls over on his back and closes his eyes, spent.

Fanny is way too excited to even close her eyes. She curls up beside Rogers, listens to his breath and waits excitedly for him to awaken.

Rogers stirs twenty minutes later. He looks fondly at Fanny and starts to roll on top of her. But a terrified look crosses Fanny's face. She stops Rogers, grips his shoulders and looks hard into his eyes.

"What is it?" says the senator.

"Are you going to fire me?"

CHAPTER 15

Nick likes being a set photographer. It's kind of like acting. One minute he is a lanky guy in a starched shirt who lost his love and the next minute—presto—there he is, camera in hand, shooting a hundred photos at a time of his old college friend.

Okay, maybe Hildy couldn't act to save her life. But she sure takes a great picture.

Unfortunately, she keeps making goo goo eyes at Nick, which interferes with his work. Not to mention endless discussions in her trailer over her "look."

She sits Nick down on the couch next to her and stares deep into his eyes. "Isn't there anything you'd like to do?" she purrs.

Nick considers the possibilities.

It's true that it could be fun to romp around with Hildy. And yet...Nick doesn't want trouble. Or a romp really. What he wants is Elizabeth. And she is gone.

Mourning his ex isn't the most manly thing Nick might do when alone in a trailer with his old college cock tease whose robe keeps slipping open, but his heart just isn't in it.

"I have an idea," she muses, "why don't we give those old coals a stir."

Nick takes a deep breath.

"Hildy," he says, "let's try to stay focused here. I should be just a fly on the wall. Catching your lightning in a bottle, so to speak. Any distractions and I might miss it."

"My lightning. I like that." Hildy inches closer. Nick feels the heat of her body through his cleanly pressed button-down.

But neither his muse nor his cock is aroused.

Could this turn into something if Hildy would just keep her purring to a minimum, her fetching little body covered up, and stop reaching for him every time she wants to make her point, whatever that is? Maybe.

Fortunately, there's a knock at her trailer door and the question is tabled.

An AD breaks through this magic moment by calling Hildy back to the set. Nick grabs his camera and follows her out of the trailer, across the street, and into an apartment where a camera unit is crammed into a corner of a first-floor living room.

Hildy joins her co-star, Laurent, on the couch facing the camera. Nick squeezes onto a windowsill and stands up to get a clear view of the couple on the couch. He puts his camera to his eye as the assistant director yells "Action!"

Hildy takes a deep breath and, eyes filling with tears, says, "I don't know why. I couldn't stop myself because I *wasn't* myself. The next thing I knew I was in the water."

Laurent puts a consoling arm around her. "Wasn't it lucky I was on the quay."

"Yes," replies Hildy. "Otherwise I'd be dead."

Until the director calls *Cut!*, Nick keeps snapping away.

CHAPTER 16

Fanny is in over her head. She is intoxicated by Lee Rogers.

It's not the senator's power she cares about either, but the truth. (At 18, you can actually think things like this without feeling pretentious or, for that matter, laughing at yourself.) There is a truth to her connection with the senator. The words "true love" come to life as she thinks about this.

Honestly, she had no intention of sleeping with Lee Rogers. And, had anyone suggested to her when she started that this is where matters would end, she would have thought it gross.

It is true that the word *Bashert* passed through Fanny's mind when she first met Lee in the airport. The word, according to a friend whose mother studied Jewish mysticism, refers to one's intended, her other half, the man that makes the woman complete. It is also true that Fanny felt something, a vague chemical heat, when she confronted Rogers in the Scranton Hotel.

But he lives in a different world. The world of politics—of smoke and mirrors and endless spin, all of which, Fanny knows, is a nice way of saying "lies." Ironic, Fanny realizes, given her interest in truth.

Fanny started her personal essay when applying to Barnard with the sentences, "I want to see, really see, the truth behind things. The naked truth." And she meant it. Her interest in documentary filmmaking and videography were all part of this same drive.

Now Fanny has seen the naked truth about Lee Rogers. Funny. And a little scary.

When she mentally replays the evening in the hotel suite with

Lee, she feels a little embarrassed. Why did she gush so freely, telling the senator about *Bashert* and the mystical connection she felt when they first met in the airport? She braces herself with the idea that love is the one thing in the whole world it is absolutely worth making a fool of yourself for.

He is married and older. Yes. But these facts dissolve in the sweetness of feelings and the intensity of the connection she senses. The pressure of Lee's hand in hers is all she needs to remind herself that the marriage and all else will somehow resolve and that, even if they don't, everything will somehow be okay.

Fanny cringes when she imagines what her mother would think if she knew. Jenny is the happiest person Fanny ever met. But Jenny would not be happy about Lee. Not at all.

The married man part is bad enough. The senator part is worse. Jenny wanted her daughter to live her own life fully and absolutely. She would hate to know that Jenny, Barnard First-Year, has wound up in the bed of a Washington power player. And the older man part, forget about it.

The only discouraging word Jenny ever said to Fanny about a boy was about Rick, the senior who wanted to take Fanny to the prom when she was a sophomore. "Stick with guys your own age, Fan. I mean it. Men are difficult enough. Older ones who prey on younger girls. I don't like that at all."

I wont tell her, Fanny thinks, relishing the feeling—the autonomy—that comes with imagining actually keeping something from her mom. Fanny can't think of a thing she hasn't shared with her mom. She told her all about how lost and confused she was during big parts of her junior and senior years. She told her, too, about losing her virginity to Mark the month before graduation, and also about how it was fine when that relationship ended.

"He was nice. But I want more than nice," she told her mom.

Go girl, said Jenny, encouraging as always.

The relationship with Lee is something different. Something that she doesn't want to share. Not simply because her mom would disapprove but also because it isn't something that she can explain, to her mom or anyone else. It's hers, just hers. The secrecy adds to the intense near-sacredness of the connection. It belongs to Jenny and to Lee in a private world—a world beyond spin, family and all else.

Naturally, Fanny has considered the possibility that she might get hurt. It's a risk she's willing to take. She was looking for truth, and she found it. In the form, in the body, in the soul of the most unlikely person. And yet.

Rogers regards Fanny's declarations with equanimity.

"How can a married man make you complete?" he asks with genuine-seeming curiosity. He listens with interest as Fanny explains herself.

"Maybe so," he tells her. "But for now...we must be discreet."

Fanny's irrepressible earnestness again: "Lee, if you ask me to, I can walk out this door and you will never see me again."

"I don't want you to leave. Just be patient. And know that I will always do the right thing. I promise." He pulls Fanny against his chest and kisses her tenderly. "You can trust me."

"I know I can," Fanny says, and then she melts into the senator's kiss.

CHAPTER 17

The bus speeds through the desert. The older woman in the seat next to Elizabeth stirs. Her head bounces and flops, like one of those drugstore dogs on a spring, and lands on Elizabeth's shoulder. Elizabeth nudges the woman away. Not gently enough. The woman wakes up.

"I'm so sorry, I've been dozing off—on you. Forgive me."

"Not a problem. You're light as a feather." Elizabeth, on her own for just a few days, has already developed an edge.

"How long have I been asleep?"

"An hour, maybe."

"Do you know where we are?"

"Just outside Reno."

"Jeez. It'll be four more days until I'm home."

"Where do you live?"

Why not? A little idle conversation, with an old woman. Beats going through the motions of seduction with some guy out of Vegas who is genuinely confused as to whether the conversation is going to end up in bed or not. (Yes, mister, it is, why else do you think I'm listening to you prattle on about your golf game, the jazz that means more to you than anything in the world, the novel that will bring you fame and fortune and change the way the world thinks? Darling. This is the noise we make to fill up the time between here and the not too distant moment when we'll be naked animals grunting and moaning in a world far from conversation.)

Monhegan Island, says the woman.

"Where is that?"

"Twelve miles off the southern coast of Maine. You can only get there by ferry. No cars on the island."

"Sounds like paradise."

"If you like seclusion. The whole place has a population of maybe a hundred people. Mostly painters and retired fishermen."

"Which are you?"

"Neither. Just retired—or about to be."

"From what?"

The woman, gray haired and nicely outfitted in a smart cardigan sweater set, says, "Dear Dottie."

"Dear Dottie? What's that?"

"I write the lovelorn column for the Boston *Star*. For the last thirty years! Used to run in the daily paper. Now it's online too—on the paper's website. People email from all over. But I'm done. And not a moment too soon. The letters and email I get…I don't know what to say anymore."

"What kind of letters? What kind of emails?"

"You have no idea."

"That bad?"

"Got a minute? What am I talking about, we've got days."

"How about a proper introduction," Elizabeth says, extending a hand and inventing a new name for herself on the spot. "I'm Elizabeth Black."

"Nice to meet you. I'm Lucy Wideman."

Lucy Wideman reaches in her bag and pulls out a letter.

"This one is pretty representative of the letters I've been getting for years. Kind of gets to you after a few decades. So many awful people out there. Nothing special about the piggery involved here except it got me to send in the resignation letter I'd drafted a long time ago." She hands the letter to Elizabeth, who opens it up and reads it to herself.

Dear Dottie,

I want to kill my husband. Or myself. I love Ben (not his real name). We've been married for twenty years. I put him through law school. When he finished, he decided he didn't want to be a lawyer. He wanted to be a political consultant.

So I supported him for three more years. I worked two jobs. A night job as a nurse three nights a week and a day job as an assistant to a hospital administrator.

I wanted to have a baby, very badly. Ben asked if we could wait until he'd finished law school. I got pregnant very quickly when he graduated. Ben said it was too soon. "Abort the baby, Betty," he said. This was very hard for me to do.

Then one day Ben told me he decided he didn't want children. "Sorry Betty. I don't." I'd supported him all those years thinking we would one day have the family of my dreams. "Sorry Betty" was all he would say.

I think you can guess how hard it was to work two jobs and keep myself in shape for my husband and now I had to give up my dreams. But I would have done anything for Ben. Apparently he did not feel that way about me.

He started up with his secretary after he joined up with a fancy political consulting firm. I didn't find out for years. I thought Lynette was a lovely lady. She always called on our anniversary and was very nice to me. We joked about how much she looked like a younger version of me.

Of course I had no idea she was involved with my husband. When I found out, I was devastated.

I couldn't work or sleep or eat or anything. I quit my job, got a trainer—damn it if I was going to lose my husband to some young duck! I used money I had squirreled away for the baby we never had, and used it for breast augmentation surgery.

Dottie, I looked good. And only then did I say to Ben "I love you. I love our life. I know what's been going on with you and Lynette and I don't care. I understand. Just end it. End it now. And let's go on with our life, the one we built and the one I love."

Ben cried. "Betty," he said, "I don't deserve you. I'll do whatever you say. My family matters most. I'll end it with Lynette."

And then he went to end it with Lynette—in a hotel room! Please don't ask me how I know—I know! I found the hotel bill on his credit card and when I asked about it, Ben told me: he couldn't stop himself.

Dear Dottie I am going to die. Either that or my husband and his little pop tart girlfriend die.

I know you will say, Betty, take your new augmented breasts and get someone new. But I don't want anyone but Ben.

Someone has to help.

Dear Dottie What Can I do?

> *I am,*
> *Desperate*

Please help me!

Lucy Wideman sighs. "You can see why I don't want to do this anymore. The only appropriate response to this letter is: 'Put a bullet through Ben's head.' "

"Who's going to replace you?" Elizabeth asks.

"Doesn't matter to me. Why? Do you want the job?"

Elizabeth considers. For a moment. Then she surprises them both by saying, "Yes! Yes I do."

Why not? Answering a bunch of letters under a made-up name might be fun. And she's perfectly glad to say it straight, to say "Put a bullet through Ben's head" when that's the appropriate response.

Elizabeth's been up there on Bruce Diamond's trophy shelf for long enough, it will be fun to have her say whenever she wants.

"What do I have to do?"

"Write an answer to this letter and email it to the editor, my boss. He'll read it. If he likes it—and he will, because he's tired and not so interested—he'll print it. If he doesn't like it, he'll suggest a couple of changes and email it back."

"Don't you ever meet with him?"

"He doesn't even know who I am. I'm a bank account and an email address to him. I never wanted anyone to know that I'm 'Dear Dottie.' It's nine hundred a week. You want the job?"

CHAPTER 18

There is a lot of downtime on the campaign trail. Boring. Fanny goes to the gym, reads film theorists like Grierson and McMahon, and "visits" with Rogers, who can't seem to get enough of her. God, they have a great time. And he's tickled by her ideas about truth and what we see and what we don't. But her constant presence is not appreciated by all.

Brock and other Rogers staffers try to exclude Fanny when they can. Right now, for example, they're at some staff meeting Fanny should be attending.

Fanny chalks it up to jealousy.

She opens her laptop and skypes Hart McCoy. They've been having an ongoing long-distance conversation about signifiers, meaning, vino and veritas. Fanny's approach to her videography has a lot to do with questions that have been under discussion in her Barnard documentary class and in her ongoing conversations with Hart.

"Hi, Hart. Miss me?"

"Yeah, Fans. It's real boring around here without you."

"I could say the same about here."

"What's the problem? No magic on the campaign trail?"

"If I have to spend one more night in a steel-town hotel room I think I might die! But I'm getting good stuff, don't you think?"

Deadly silence from Hart's end of the computer. Finally, he says, "I guess so." The effort required to get the words out is evident.

"You guess so? Don't you know?"

"Yeah, I know. I know someone who's lost her objectivity."

"What do you mean?"

"That bit about his shoes? Every time he looks towards the camera he's batting his eyelashes."

"Batting his eyelashes? WTF, Hart? No. He's not batting his eyelashes."

"Like I said, you've completely lost your objectivity. One question: Are you sleeping with him?"

Fanny feigns outrage. "Of course not!"

"Really. Well, tell him to stop flirting with you. Do you think he'd get that stupid grin off his face if I were shooting him?"

"I'm not so sure. You're pretty cute." Fanny tries hard to steer the conversation in jauntier directions.

"You're right about that. But I don't think good-looking young boys are his particular bent."

"Come on, Hart, you've got to be kidding."

"No, I'm not kidding. You've broken the golden rule of documentary filmmaking. You've gone native. You're captive. Totally taken in—conned—by your subject."

"I am not."

"You're hardly an objective judge of your own work."

Hart seems to be bridling up his high horse for a good trot. He's off and running, sprinkling his general denunciation with nuggets from Docs class.

"Watching your stuff is like watching *Primary*," he says, citing a classic spin job from before spin jobs were even invented. "Those Kennedys were masters of image creation. Who do you think dreamed up the whole Camelot thing?"

Hart is getting to her. Fanny wonders: *has* she lost her objectivity? Has the truth about her connection with Rogers clouded her vision of Senator Rogers, candidate?

Fanny's head is spinning.

She takes a defensive tack: "I think I've captured unique moments that you never see in campaign coverage."

"I'm surprised they're letting you post those love-isodes on their website. How does that genius campaign manager like them?"

"Not much."

"I wonder why? I hope Rogers' wife is not tuning in."

"Okay okay, Hart, I got it. I've got to go—to a meeting."

Fanny doesn't have a meeting to go to. Brock has seen to that. For a mad moment she wonders if she has, in fact, lost her head, lost her grasp on truth.

Then her phone rattles. She sees Lee's text: "I'm thinking of you, baby. Can't wait to see you tomorrow morning, early. In fact I think I'd like to have you for breakfast. Big Kiss, L."

And Hart and all his mumbo jumbo about *Primary* and objectivity fly straight out the window of Fanny's bright young mind.

CHAPTER 19

Connie Rogers has always cared about her hair. A pale shade of brown, it has begun to thin. And lighten. She worries that it has the flyaway look she sees sometimes on old women on park benches.

Connie has not yet experienced the dramatic, disrupting tremors many Parkinson's sufferers have. But even in her sturdiest days, hand-eye coordination was not her strength. Keeping her hair in the top-notch shape that befits a candidate's wife requires help.

In fact Connie is pretty sure she could live longer without her Parkinson's medications than she could without Roseanne. For thirty years—and at least thirty shades of highlights and lowlights, countless shades of brown, dark and deep blonde—Roseanne has been Connie's hair colorist and, of course, friend.

After a short weekend with Rogers in Washington, Connie takes the train home so that she can see Roseanne first thing Monday morning. She wants to have her hair right for the Lower Merion Quaker Ladies Group Monday afternoon.

The Anna Zane Salon is a small shop, just six chairs. There's a nice intimate feeling here. Connie is happy to be home with the ladies when she marches into the shop early Monday morning.

"Gorgeous day, Rosie," she says.

"Gorgeous day for some gorgeous hair. Let's get yours in shape."

Connie grabs a magazine or two—*Pennsylvia* magazine and a few old copies of *People*. She thumbs distractedly through these. Generally it's more pleasant to talk with Roseanne than to catch up on local comings and goings and celebrity gossip.

Roseanne paints Connie's head with a thick paste. In the next chair, Tina, Roseanne's associate, folds tin-foil packets of hair color onto the head of Libby Reynolds. Connie has known Libby for years. They aren't friends but they go to the same country club in the summer.

"Coffee, ladies?" says the shop assistant.

No thanks. Connie is tanked up and so, apparently is Libby, who has just run across a photo of Arnold Schwarzenegger riding a motorcycle in her old copy of *People*.

"Can you believe anyone ever elected this guy? I mean really?" says Libby. She passes the *People* to Connie.

"Hard to imagine anyone took him seriously," Tina says. "I mean, *Hasta La Vista* and all that Terminator stuff." Tina is a movie junkie.

"And let's not even get to the part about how he was banging the housekeeper all that time. I mean, really. Sleeping with the housekeeper and his wife at the same time. The guy's got two kids, two different mothers. They're running around the house together. And no one notices they look alike? Really?"

Roseanne has a great genius for the obvious. This is not a common quality. It's a rare thing to hold fast to the simple truth of things, and not cloud things up with obscuring complications, needless nuance.

"How old are those boys now?" says Connie. Connie's genius is for the straight and narrow, which is exactly where her question would turn the conversation if any cared to follow, which, of course, they do not.

"Can you imagine?" Libby says. "Two kids running around. Looking alike. It takes *twelve years* before anyone figures it out!"

"Poor Maria," says Tina.

"Dumb Maria," says Roseanne.

"Didn't she notice that Arnold messed up the house a lot so

he could call on the housekeeper's 'services'?" Ha ha. Tina is a cut-up.

"Yeah. Really great the way Arnold stayed home with the kids—and the housekeeper—so that Maria could go out and promote her career," Roseanne offers. "Ever see a picture of the housekeeper? She wasn't the most attractive person in the world. She just happened to be there."

Libby shakes her head sadly. "The wife is always the last to know."

Connie follows the conversation with interest. She flips the page. She'd rather not look at Arnold Schwarzenegger on his motorcycle anymore. And she'd rather not think about Schwarzenegger's wife, in the dark all that time.

"Hollywood. Different rules govern there," she says. "All that tinsel and glitter." She turns the page to a story about a cancer survivor who has patented an early diagnostic test.

"Oh yeah? What about that congressman?" Tina is remarkably up on current affairs. "You know the one who was on tape propositioning young pages?"

Libby remembers that scandal well too. "Yeah. But that was homosexual. Totally different," she says.

Roseanne runs her brush across Connie's scalp, filling in the spots she's missed. "I don't think it's so different." Roseanne reminds the entourage that the *Philadelphia Inquirer* reported, just last week, that Dirk Reynolds, Deputy Mayor, was carrying on with his secretary.

"Right," says Tina. "And when Coco Reynolds found out, she threw Dirk out in a heartbeat. Just as she should have."

"Dog," says Connie.

CHAPTER 20

"Guess what," Senator Rogers tells Fanny. He is sitting on another red leather sofa in another hotel suite. He has his monthly calendar on his knee. "We're going to France."

"Really?" says Fanny.

"Three days in Paris for a NATO conference," says Rogers straightening his tie. And he's off to a breakfast briefing.

Later Fanny, alone, heads into her hotel bathroom. She's wearing a white terry robe emblazoned with the Marriott logo over black jeans and a tank top. She's shooting her reflection in the bathroom mirror.

"Paris!" she says to the camera in the mirror. "How great! Meanwhile, things are getting a little weird around here. I'm getting funny looks *all* the time. Especially when Lee and I are laughing together. They resent my closeness to him. He says I'm paranoid, nothing's changed, just do your job, blah dee blah dee da."

There's a knock at the door. Fanny turns the camera off, tightens the bathrobe belt, walks through the hotel room and opens the door. It's Brock. "Can I come in and have a word with you," he says. Stern. No jokes. Not even a pleasant remark about the rainy Lancaster morning.

"Sure," says Fanny. "Is something wrong?"

"Maybe," says Brock. All business. "You know the Philly *Star*?"

Fanny does not know the Philly *Star* and thinks, momentarily, about astronomy.

"It's a rag. And they're poking around, asking questions about you and Lee."

"But why?"

"Um, let's see," says Brock. "A good-looking girl follows him around with a camera all the time? Questions arise."

"But it's my job!" Fanny and her usual big-time earnestness.

"Listen, Fanny. It doesn't look good. With his wife sick and not traveling with him on the campaign. They're picking up gossip. And gossip goes right on their front page whether it's true or not. Now with the last debate coming up, I don't want anything muddying the waters or scotching our chances. You see what I'm saying?"

"I'm so sorry," says Fanny, "I didn't mean to hurt Lee in any…"

"I know that, Fanny. It's just appearances, okay?" He's softening Fanny for a blow that she sees coming.

"So what do you want me to do? Disappear?"

Eureka, thinks Brock. *That was easy*.

"Just until we get past Tuesday and clinch the final debate," he tells Fanny. "And I want you to know from me directly, you've been a big part of the campaign's uptick."

Brock hugs Fanny and leaves. *Mission accomplished*, he thinks as he heads towards the elevator.

Fanny walks through the bedroom, where she left the camcorder, and takes it back into the bathroom. She thumbs the power and resumes shooting herself in the mirror.

"Where do men learn to lie like that?"

CHAPTER 21

The Lower Merion Quaker Ladies Group might as well be the Altoona School Parents Organization. Or the Harrisburg Women's Bar Association.

Connie Rogers has been to a million of these. She loves each and every one of them. A chance to meet new people, listen to new ideas, shake hands and most of all to talk about Senator Lee Rogers.

Connie's energy is flagging, slightly, from the medication and maybe the weight loss, but she's just as game as always. (And besides, her clothes fit better!)

After tea and talk and what Connie regards as a hopeful sign of interest from a potential big campaign donor, she stops to chat with the small clique of Rogers' staff people who've stayed behind.

Lily, Nanci ("with an *i*"), and Bob are long-time members of the Rogers team, practically family, really. They're chatting about the weekend, polling data and increased traffic on the *Lee Rogers for Senate* campaign website when Connie enters the conversation.

"They're fun," says Nanci. "They really do provide a look at Lee in action. You know, in a becoming, not so stiff, candidate-y way."

"Not sure if the webisodes are what's driving the traffic up or not," Bob says. "But they are fun. And maybe they show voters another side of Lee."

"I know!" Lily agrees. "Who knew Lee cared about whether his shoes are cool are not?" She sees Connie and makes room for her to join the circle. "I thought you bought Lee all his clothes, Connie. Because he doesn't care at all about clothes or shoes or what's cool."

No, Connie thinks, *he doesn't*.

She wonders what these "webisodes" are and why Lee is using them to broadcast some weird new interest in fashion.

No sooner is Connie home than she heads into the library, boots up the computer and types *RogersforSenate.com* into Google.

There it is, all the way on the right: *Webisodes*.

Connie clicks. There's Lee, smiling at the camera, talking about foreign policy and...shoes. He looks odd. Giddy and vaguely flirtatious as he talks into the camera asking questions about what's cool.

Connie sees the words "About the Webisodes" at the bottom of the screen and clicks. A sick electric jolt climbs up her throat when a picture of Fanny, with a camcorder in her hand, flashes up on the screen.

"Lee, we have to talk," she says into the receiver when she reaches him on his private cell phone.

Really this couldn't be a worse time for Rogers. "I'm sorry, darling. Very busy here. Working on the mass incarceration criminal justice reform speech. Could I call later?"

"No, Lee. Now."

Is she having new symptoms? Lee has rarely heard this level of alarm in Connie's voice. "The webisode thing. That web girl. Lee. Are you...carrying on with her?"

Rogers laughs. Ha ha ha. "Connie, are you okay? Of course I'm not 'carrying on.' With the web girl, Franny, or whatever her name is—or anyone else."

"Tell me the truth, Lee. I can take it." In truth, Connie is not at all sure she can take it, whatever it is.

"Darling. Please. Are you taking the Sinemet? Confusion and paranoia *are* side effects."

"I'm sick, Lee. I'm sick. But I don't have extreme symptoms. And I haven't had side effects from the meds. I saw the videos and you seemed so…strange."

"Connie, my love. You know what's coming up? Our thirtieth anniversary! I love you, darling. You and you alone. I have to be in Paris for a NATO conference. What do you say you come along. We can renew our vows on top of the Eiffel Tower! Oh, let's do it, Connie! The campaign is hard on all of us, especially you, in your condition. Look what you've dreamt up. Let me take you away from all this. At least for a few days. We'll renew our vows, eat some ace food, and knock all this kooky stuff out of your head."

Rogers is surprised by this torrent of unexpected declarations. And the invitation to Paris. Nice touch. He's at his best under pressure, always has been.

For a half a second Connie wonders if it is the medication— Doctor Katz did say it could cause paranoia, even hallucinations —and then she's racing off in her mind to the closet, wondering what she'll pack for the Paris trip and whether it will interfere with her scheduled fundraisers and campaign briefings.

"That shoe thing threw me. I'm silly. And I'm sorry. I love you. Count me in for the Eiffel Tower trip."

"Don't worry about it, darling. I'm here for you. Always."

"All right, dear. Forgive me. Pay no attention. Go back to your work, Lee. I love you."

CHAPTER 22

Elizabeth sits in front of a bay window in a one-bedroom cottage overlooking the rocky Maine coast. The water is ice cold. Swimming is not on today's schedule. Neither is talking to anyone since there isn't really anyone around. Elizabeth lolls in the delicious expanse of empty space.

Elizabeth sits herself down at an old wooden table, pulls up her chair and opens her laptop. Now she's Dottie.

> *Dear Dottie,*
>
> *I know my boyfriend loves me very much. But he's been acting screwy lately and he tells me he slept with someone he had a crush on in high school. He said he was scared he'd wrecked the best thing in his life and could I forgive him? I can. He's bipolar. If he readjusts his dosages and stops drinking, he'll see clearly and come back.*
>
> *I love him very much.*
>
> *Should I be tough or just give him the care and love he needs?*
>
> > *Yours,*
> > *Fighting Hard*

Elizabeth rolls her eyes.

> *Dear Fighting Hard,*
>
> *Do the words "lost cause" mean anything to you?*
>
> *Cheating on you and blaming it on mental illness—that's as low as you can get.*
>
> *Bipolar? What else is this pond scum? Let me guess. Alcoholic? Really boring? A Nazi?*

Fighting Hard, you're fighting the truth.
Strychnine is the only medicine for this creep.

Yours,
Dottie

Elizabeth is having fun. The inbox is full of queries and, so far, no one in the home office has objected to—or maybe noticed—"Dottie's" new tone.

Other people's problems are soooo easy, Elizabeth thinks.

She rifles through a terrible assortment of letters from people with all kinds of maladies, broken hearts, incurable diseases, murderous secrets, you name it.

What is the matter with these people? Elizabeth asks herself as she clicks open a letter from someone who calls herself "It Wont Be Long":

Dear Dottie.

> *I have terminal cancer. I hadn't seen my ex-husband in 18 months. But, when he heard I was in the hospital, he showed up and started asking questions about my estate and has been suggesting I have a living will and all kinds of things like that.*
>
> *I don't have any children or family. The hospital is very crowded and staff is short and I can't get painkillers or any help really unless someone is here with me.*
>
> *My ex scares me—also I hate him—and it looks like he's angling in on my estate. But I need him now. What do you think? Is there anything wrong with letting him care for me now?*

Signed,
It Wont Be Long

Elizabeth thinks this is definitely getting to be a bit much.

Dear It Wont Be Long,

Really? Has the cancer gone to your head?

Get rid of this jerk before he pulls your plug.

If you've got money, you can pay someone else to be with you in the hospital.

Jack the Ripper sounds like a safer bet than this vampire.

Yours,

Dottie

After a few more days of this, the bloom is off the Dear Dottie business.

"Man, there are a lot of sad dumb people out there." Elizabeth has taken to talking to herself—and to the turtles outside.

Lying low sucks.

CHAPTER 23

On a sunny Paris afternoon, Nick enjoys a citron pressé with Lester, a photographer friend. A burly man in his mid-40's and in a plaid flannel shirt, Lester takes pictures for tabloid newspapers. He's good at hiding behind potted plants and parked cars.

At the vaguest whiff of a celebrated nose or leg or expensively redone cheekbone Lester uncoils, like a snake, and starts snapping.

"Who do you think comes to a NATO conference?" Lester wants to know.

Nick states the obvious. "Middle-aged blowhards come to NATO conferences. Actually," Nick corrects himself, "ancient blowhards. Hard to believe you can sell pictures of any of them. Unless, of course, they come with Ashley Dupré or one of her cousins."

"Yup. As always, the wives, the girlfriends, the hookers, those are the only prospects." Lester sips his citron pressé and changes gears. "How's the film going?" he asks.

"Barely. They've been rained out at the Eiffel Tower so they went to cover."

"Cover?" It's an American expression Lester doesn't know.

"Where you go when you need bright sunshine and it's raining."

"So what's the cover today?"

"A mental institution," Nick says. "Laurent has a breakdown after Hildy goes off the tower."

Lester manages to avoid rolling his eyes. The movie business! What chaos. Best to just change the subject.

"Have you done any work on your book?"

Nick is all earnestness. "Remember that girl, Elizabeth, that vanished in Vegas? I still think there could be an idea there."

Lester does his best not to look dubious. "Hmm," he says. "What's the story?"

"Right now," says Nick, "I haven't got one. But I took a ton of pictures."

"Maybe," suggests Lester, "you need a new girl that has a story. You know. One with a beginning, a middle and an end." Who wants to see a bunch of pictures of some girl that don't add up to anything? Where's the payoff?

"Thing is, you can't know the end of a new girl's story," Nick says, "until she's not a new girl anymore. And most stories don't have great endings."

"What do you consider a great ending?" Lester asks.

"Well," Nick says, "*Vertigo*'s got a great one. The picture I'm working on. Maybe the greatest ending of all time."

Sure, Nick knows: most people zone out when you tell them movie plots. Same thing when someone starts talking about their dreams. Zzzzzzz. Goodnight. Thanks for sharing.

But Lester's not going anywhere unless, of course, Kate Moss or Carla Bruni walk by.

"Okay. Here you go. In *Vertigo* a man is madly in love with a mysterious woman. He follows her around because her husband thinks she's possessed by someone named Carlotta, some distant relative who killed herself a long time ago. The guy worries that his beautiful wife is going to kill herself on the same day Carlotta died. She keeps talking about the tower where Carlotta jumped to her death. Our hero realizes there is a real tower just like the one she describes. He takes her there to show her that it's real, not some phantom in her crazed imagination. But when they get there, she runs away from him and up the steps of the tower."

"Sounds like he's a big dope," Lester says. "He led her to her doom, right?"

"Right," Nick continues. He's intense. "She climbs to the top of the tower. It's pretty clear she's going to jump."

Lester says, "Why doesn't he run up after her?"

"Remember the name of the movie? *Vertigo.* Guess who's got it? Plus acrophobia, fear of heights. He can't even look at the steps without getting dizzy and starting to black out."

"Okay," Lester says, "so she jumps. He can't save her. He feels guilty the rest of his life." Lester shrugs. "That's a great ending? Really?"

"No, no, no." Nick doles out the real ending for Lester as if he were spooning him chocolate mousse. "It turns out she's not really the wife. She's just pretending to be. The husband knows our guy *can't* climb steps. He killed his real wife, and when the fake one gets to the top, he throws the real one over the edge. Voila! Now he has the perfect witness to his wife's 'suicide.' Complicated. But great. Takes a little work to think it through."

Lester isn't listening. He's still thinking about Nick's problem. "What about that girl in your picture, Hildy? You must have a slew of pictures of her by now."

"She's an old love story that doesn't need retelling. I need to feel the rush and shoot it."

Lester stares off into space. "I remember the rush. I'm still making the child support payments."

CHAPTER 24

Rogers is in the bathroom, running the water. He's finishing a shave. Slowly, over the running water, he registers the sound of Fanny sobbing quietly in the expensive sheets in the big bed in the guest room of the Washington townhouse. (Rogers would never have another woman in the bed he shares with Connie.)

"You promised. You promised." She makes sad little sounds in between sobs.

Rogers walks out of the bathroom in a towel.

"She's coming, Fanny. And there's not a damn thing I can do about it," says Rogers. Seeing him naked from the waist up, Fanny recalls that Rogers is known, to Senate staffers, as the Hunk of the Hill.

The Hunk of the Hill is a heap of swill, thinks Fanny, giving herself a momentary reprieve from her tears, her fury.

"When are you going to tell her about us," she asks Rogers. He sits beside her on the bed.

The hunk, the hulk, he twists his bulk. And screws his mouth into something like a sneer.

"Oh, that's a great idea, Fanny. A great, great idea. In an election year, why don't I break it to my wife that it's over, my wife of thirty years, my wife who is standing behind me while she's dying? I can just break it to her on a romantic stroll along the Seine. Or maybe I can call a press conference and tell the whole fucking world."

Fanny is taken aback. She rarely sees the business end of the senator's moods. "But you said you loved me! And you promised you'd tell her."

The senator reins in the rage. He's a guy who's made a career of concessions. "I will, Fanny, but not in Paris. I can't. I proposed to her in Paris. Thirty years ago. On the top of the Eiffel Tower."

"Oh that's romantic." Look! Fanny and Rogers are taking turns with mockery and put-downs, playing a zippy game of emotional ping-pong.

The senator is surprised to see Fanny ace a shot with withering sarcasm. He softens. "Wait until we get back. I promise I'll tell her then. Now, be a good girl and get dressed."

Fanny decides not to be a good girl. Instead she picks up a framed picture of the senator and his wife and throws it at him.

The senator ducks—fast reflexes—and it smashes against the wall behind him. Broken glass showers the floor.

"What do you think you're doing? That's one of Connie's favorite pictures!"

He's never been this angry with her before. But when Fanny gets out of bed and stands, naked, before him, his fury dissolves. The old hunger stirs in his loins. *So what? She broke a picture.*

"Oh, honey," he says, all milk and honey. "I'm so sorry. She never goes to these things. But suddenly, out of the blue, this time she changed her mind. And after the conference, I have to get right back, this damn defense appropriation bill is up for another vote and—" He's exhausted. But what he says next *is* true: "You know how much I need you…I just can't do anything about it now."

Fanny half whimpers. "You *say* that, but you *never* do anything about it!"

"Fanny, Fanny, Fanny. Once this is settled, I'll talk to her. We'll fix this—"

Fanny marches into the bathroom. It begins to dawn on her

that she has become a cliché, a camp follower in love with a married politician who, like the rest, lives on lies in the shadows.

She dries her eyes on a particularly fluffy white towel. She looks at herself in the mirror with fresh eyes. "Hello, cliché," she says to herself.

Then Fanny watches herself gather composure. She holds her head up, gives herself a shot of her expensive perfume (Déjà Vu!), gives the towel a shot for good measure (a little something to remind him of her, when she's gone), and smelling like a gardenia and peonies, hint of citrus, Fanny walks back into the bedroom with a solemn face.

"Goodbye, Lee. I'm out of here. And I'm not coming back." She's not kidding. A phone call to her mom and she'll be on the first plane back to San Francisco, courtesy of Loft Airlines.

San Francisco? With Mom?

She'll think of something…

Rogers reaches for her and tries to pull her close.

"*No*," she says and pushes him away. She slams her foot down on the floor. Her foot meets a glass shard from the broken photo frame. "Shit!"

The senator rushes over, tries to comfort her, but she stops him in his tracks with a death glare.

"Where are you going to go, Fanny? What are you going to do?"

Is that concern in his voice, or is it anxiety?

Fanny limps to the bed, finds her underwear in the pile, starts putting it on. She's got three or four smart answers on the tip of her tongue, but sometimes silence cuts deeper. Like a piece of glass to your tender sole.

Let him suffer. Let him wonder if he'll ever see me again.

Later that night Fanny is seated on a night flight to Paris. Her eyes are red from crying. She takes a little pill case out of her purse, dumps four tablets into her hand, and drops them into her mouth. She washes them down with a mini-bar size bottle of gin. She puts her earphones in place and listens to a Rosetta Stone tape. "Bonjour!" she says with a boozy slur. "Est-ce que vous avez une chaise?...Je n'aimer pas la moutarde."

And then she falls fast asleep. Bon Nuit Fanny.

CHAPTER 25

Jenny Cours could not be more excited. Fanny arrives home tonight, from D.C.

She sounded rushed on the phone, said she wanted to get away—fast. Jenny booked her a trip back to San Francisco, texted her the departure information, didn't hear anything further, and had no reason to think Fanny wouldn't show up. She always did.

Jenny was on the threshold of middle age when Fanny began to burst into womanly bloom. Jenny got a kick out of this. Without envy or regret, she celebrated her daughter's impossible beauty and bright prospects.

But Jenny doesn't wish she were 18 again. Genuinely happy with herself and the choices she has made, Jenny looks on aging with pleasure and interest. *This will be fun*, she thinks, *a whole new world.* Jenny enjoys herself every bit as much at 45 as she did at 25. She likes the way she feels, lives and looks. Take that, everybody else.

Right now, Jenny is just looking forward to Fanny's arrival. At the last moment, she decided a surprise welcome committee of one very happy mom would make Fanny's homecoming that much more festive.

In fact, Jenny was so looking forward to Fanny's arrival, she wasn't sure what to do with herself. She's already filled the house with tulips, Fanny's favorite flowers, and spent hours preparing Veau de Blanc, Fanny's favorite dinner.

It's funny to watch the passengers deplane into the concourse. Jenny, who has seen this scene a million times from the reverse vantage, feels a little like she's fallen through an Alice-in-Wonderland hole in the world.

She watches the first-class passengers roll their expensive bags past. Then come the business-class folks with their less expensive bags. Weird that America created such a rigid class system in the sky.

All digressive thought fades when the economy-class passengers began to deplane and Jenny focuses her complete attention on Fanny, or rather on trying to find Fanny in the crowd.

Fanny, however, does not get off the plane.

Worse, when Jenny, confused and also concerned, inquires, she is horrified to learn that no one named Fanny Cours ever boarded the plane from D.C.

CHAPTER 26

Le Métro speeds under the Paris streets.

The car has the vacant feel that subways all over the world have late at night.

Nick, Lester and Jean, a middle-aged French reporter for *Paris Match*, have been drinking. It must have been a lot or the bumps along the way wouldn't trouble their stomachs as much as they do. Jean's especially.

Aside from Jean (now hiccupping) and his buddies there is one other guy, unshaven and kind of creepy looking, in the car. (Not that anyone looks good under fluorescent métro car lights. Do they get special bulbs designed to make everyone look their worst or what?)

Mister Unshaven-and-kind-of-creepy-looking eyes the shapeless brown wool coat on the seat across from him. A bit of movement reveals that the coat is attached to a pair of legs. Shapely legs. Shapely legs in black tights and black army boots.

This image catches Nick's eye and he instinctively takes out his iPhone and snaps a few pictures.

A strange jumble of words—are they French?—emerge from the tangled coat, which Nick now sees covers not just a pair of legs and a girl, but also a canvas travel bag with a handle and wheels.

Jean rubs his eyes. "I have to get up early, guys. Big perfume powwow this week." He yawns and hiccups at the same time. "Why do I let you talk me into these things?"

"Nothing ventured, nothing gained," says Lester. "The girls in there looked good at the time."

The coat rolls over on the opposite seat and guess who is under it? Red-eyed Fanny. She tries to adjust the empty coat sleeve over her head as she struggles to sit up. Her attempt is not even remotely successful.

Jean gives Lester a nudge. "Too bad the girls in the bar didn't look like that," he says, directing Lester's attention to Fanny; a little disheveled, she is, in fact, no less fetching for all that.

"Yeah," says Lester, "too bad. Think of all the money we would have saved if they looked like that and showed up drunk out of their minds."

Jean looks at his watch. "Mon dieu! I'm not going to be worth a shit in the morning," he says.

Lester is bored with Jean and his bellyaching. He looks away, studies the creepy guy and the girl on the opposite seat. The creepy guy stares blankly. Fanny, clearly very drunk, rolls over and goes back to sleep under her coat.

The train pulls into the station. Lester gets up to leave and Jean, apparently struck by a memory that this is his stop too, gets up to go as well. Nick pockets his iPhone and stands. His stop is next.

Lester eyes Fanny (or more exactly, her coat) and the creepy guy as he makes his way towards the door. "Keep an eye on her. She has another admirer," he tells Nick. The doors slide shut behind him.

Nick, relieved to be free of his buddies, looks over and sees that the unshaven guy has shifted his attention from Fanny's legs to her bag.

When the train pulls into the next station, he steps off the car and onto a deserted platform. No one boards the train.

Nick is about to head towards the exit when, through the train window, he sees the scruffy man move towards Fanny.

Nick shakes his head and runs back on just as the doors start to close.

He walks over to the seat where Fanny lies, still fast asleep.

The shady and vaguely threatening character registers Nick's presence, walks past Fanny, and pretends to check the Métro Map posted on the wall behind her. It's obvious to Nick that the directions the guy is looking for—the fastest path to Fanny's bag —are not on the map.

Nick moves in front of Fanny to get her attention. He fails. He nudges her leg. She rouses slightly, pushes the hair out of her eyes and smiles.

"Est-ce que je puis vous aider?" Nick is nothing if not polite.

Sadly the motion required to listen upsets Fanny's precarious balance. As the train lurches around a corner, she starts to slide off the seat.

Nick grabs hold of her and keeps her from falling.

"Bonjour!" Fanny says brightly.

"Hey." Nick rolls Fanny onto her back. "Hey! Wake up!"

Fanny smiles sweetly. "Je n'aimer pas la moutarde," she says.

"I don't like it either," Nick says, "C'mon. Wake up. If the cops find you like this, you're going to wind up in jail."

Fanny regards Nick with interest. "Hey, you speak English. Are we in England?"

"No," says Nick flatly, "we're not in England. We're in Paris. But everyone in Paris isn't French."

Fanny smiles sweetly, again. "Ought to be a law against that," she says.

"Law against what?" Nick wonders why he is having this conversation.

Fanny tries to grab her train of thought before it chugs off. "A law against being in France and not being French."

"Well, there isn't."

"Hey," she says. "Did you say something about a cop?"

Nick nods. Fanny wavers a little. She isn't fully awake, but she's interested. "Where is that cop?" she wonders.

Nick remembers longingly that he was on his way back to his hotel, to bed. "You know, people who can't drink...shouldn't."

The train slows to a stop.

"This is where we get off," Nick tells her. He puts his arm around her and helps her off the train. He eases her and her bag gingerly down the platform, up the steps and onto the street.

The Rue Saint-Honoré has a beautiful fairytale look; car lights glitter in the empty dark. Nick sets Fanny on a bench—she'll love the view—and whistles for a cab.

"Get yourself some coffee. You'll be okay," he tells her as he gets into the car.

He looks back and sees she's flopped over and is lying on the bench. The driver sees her too. It doesn't look good.

Nick returns to the bench and tries to stir Fanny. "Go ahead," he tells her, "you take the cab. I'll walk." Fanny doesn't move. The driver toots his horn.

Fanny sees it. She gets a giddy look. "Le taxi!" she says.

"Yes. Le taxi," Nick says dryly. "I can drop you off. Where are you staying?"

"The Eiffel Tower," says Fanny. And giggles.

Nick is having something like a bad dream. "C'mon. You're not *that* drunk. Where's your room?"

"Drunk!" says Fanny. "I'm not drunk at all." She drops her head on Nick's chest. "I'm just verrrry haaaaaapy. When I should be verrrry sad. Isn't that smart?"

Brilliant. Totally brilliant, Nick thinks. The driver tells Nick it's late, he needs to get the cab home. Where should he take the young man and his friend?

Fanny is sound asleep again when the cab pulls up at Nick's

hotel. He takes her bag and her arm and, in something a lot like a sleepwalk, she trails him up the steps.

"Is this the elevator?" Fanny asks when he opens the door to his room. Nick tells her no, it's his hotel room. Fanny bumps into the bed, grabs the headboard to steady herself. "How many of you are there in the room?" she asks Nick.

"One," he says.

"Well, that's one good thing," she says, looking around. "Can I sleep here?"

Nick tells Fanny that is the general idea and she flops onto the bed. Nick walks over to the table by the front door, pours himself a Jack Daniels and swallows it. He puts the glass down and goes over to Fanny and the bed.

"Are you going to sleep with me?" she says.

"No," says Nick, "I like my girls…conscious."

This strikes Fanny as a perfectly reasonable preference. She turns over onto her stomach and passes out.

CHAPTER 27

Lee Rogers is in bed with his wife.

The air conditioner hums through the Rogers home. All is cool and tidy inside the four-story Georgetown townhouse.

Lee's career has been foremost in Connie's mind for more years than she can remember. The house is a showcase for his achievement. It is stately, grand and smells, vaguely, of money.

Connie has decorated the house in what is called a traditional style. The tradition apparently involves horses, dogs, bourbon and men who speak in hushed voices about things that seem to matter a lot and either do or else don't matter at all.

Connie's money, the money that's paid for the house, is Jewish money. But you could not guess this from the look of things here.

There is a careful collection of photos in the front parlor. These show Rogers shaking hands with innumerable dignitaries and all five living Presidents.

There are also photos of the Rogers children, Willa and Deron, jumping horses and running dogs on the Maryland shore. They do not show pictures of Deron entering the Silver Hill mental health facility where his parents sent him to recover from a drug habit.

Heroin. Heroin. Never in a hundred years would Connie or Lee Rogers have imagined their child, a private school graduate who spent summers at Echo Hill, would have a drug problem, a heroin habit.

Most painful—or shocking—of all to Connie was that she had no idea Deron was in trouble; he left college and went west to California where, Connie thought, he got a job as a paralegal and enrolled in an LSAT course. How could she possibly have been so completely in the dark as to what was going on in her own family?

Connie did not believe Willa when she called, months later, to say Deron was not in a paralegal program, was not studying for the LSAT, and was not living in the Pacific Heights apartment for which his parents sent him $2,900 per month for rent. He was in fact living in a cheap SRO in the Tenderloin and using the rent money to support his new habit.

Connie did not want to tell the senator at first. She worried that the discovery might interfere with Lee's work, his image, the re-election prospects around which family life had long been centered.

Connie and Willa flew to San Francisco and persuaded Deron to get help. Doctors recommended Silver Hill. It was only after Deron was admitted that Connie told the senator.

"I am sorry to hear you have had a bad patch of it and will support you always," Lee said to Deron on the phone when he called him moments after his admission. An outsider would have been forgiven for thinking that Lee was calling a candidate for Congress to wish him well after a bad bout of publicity.

Deron recovered in time (and after much expense) and Connie and Lee tacitly colluded in the collective effort to make Deron's "problem" disappear from family memory. Two years later he was back West, in Petaluma, working on a horse farm.

Connie sometimes wondered after that if he might be in trouble again but never said so and most definitely never asked; at family gatherings, Connie spoke to her son mostly about horses and the Senate. The whole mess brought Connie and Rogers closer together. It cemented an ongoing conspiracy between them.

Lee and Connie's bedroom has the cozy, well-appointed

warmth of a high-end hotel room. Much thought has gone into creating the general sense that everything is in order.

This order is disturbed now by a ringing phone. Lee switches on the light. He says, "Hello, who is it?" into the phone, in the voice of someone expecting a call at 1AM.

"It's Jenny Cours," says the voice on the other end. "Lee. I'm sorry to wake you. I'm worried about Fanny. Very worried."

"Fanny?" says Rogers. He is suddenly very alert. "What about Fanny?"

Connie, rail thin and full of Parkinson's medications, stirs slightly and inches closer to her husband.

Jenny says she does not want to panic. But Fanny was supposed to be home, in Menlo Park, this evening. She didn't show up.

"Something's wrong." Jenny's voice is as tense as he's ever heard it.

Rogers sits upright in his pressed blue broadcloth pajamas. He is the picture of reassurance. He pats his wife's drowsy head. "Now take it easy," he says. "Maybe she missed her flight. It's probably something simple like that. Kids. Lots going on."

"No," Jenny says, "she would have called. She always calls. Or texts."

Jenny is increasingly frantic. The fact that she's calling is, in fact, a sign of how frantic she is. She never called Lee at home, even when they were seeing each other twenty years ago.

Jenny says she's checked all of the airlines and there is no record of Fanny traveling.

"I begged her not to work on your campaign," she says, concentrating her worry into a dart she throws in the senator's face. "I knew something like this would happen. Lee. Please. I need your help."

Connie gets up to go to the bathroom. Her gown is white

with roses. Half asleep as she pulls herself out of the bed, Connie regards her husband with affection and mild concern. Late-night phone calls are not uncommon; Connie is proud her husband is vitally involved in so many important matters. And yet, that name. This particular important late-night matter involves that girl, Fanny.

"I'll make some calls and see what I can find out," Rogers says as the bathroom door shuts behind Connie with a click.

He hears Jenny break into tears. "I'm sorry, Lee," she says. (Why do crying women always apologize?) "Fanny means everything to me. She's so reliable. I can't believe I haven't heard from her. I keep thinking of that girl, the intern in Rock Creek Park."

"Come on, Jenny. Calm. Let me see what I can find out," says Rogers. "We'll find her. I'll call you when I find out what's what."

Rogers hangs up the phone and quickly dials another number. He is thankful that Connie is still in the bathroom when he reaches Brock.

"Get over here, Bart. I need some help," he says.

A few minutes later, Connie returns to bed. "Something at work?" she murmurs as she pulls back the covers. She is so proud of her husband, so pleased to think his recent ranking membership in the Committee on Foreign Relations will help his campaign. So hopeful that this late-night call is nothing.

"Mm-hm," says Rogers, slipping quietly out of bed and into the dressing room. He hangs the broadcloth pajamas on a hook, outfits himself in khakis and polo shirt and goes downstairs to wait for Brock.

CHAPTER 28

The senator's cleanup man arrives in khakis and a polo shirt. If Rogers weren't agitated, he would find this comical. But he is agitated and says nothing about the fact that the men are in matching outfits.

"When was the last time you saw her?" Brock asks. He sips the coffee Rogers has brought him.

"Two nights ago." Rogers is crisp and to the point. He anticipates the next question. "I saw her here."

Brock is not surprised. He has not forgotten the circumstances under which the two men first met.

"Who knows about her?" Brock asks. He is skeptical when Rogers says absolutely no one knows.

"She didn't tell a soul," Rogers insists. "She knew all the staffers gossip. She was determined not to make the same mistakes." It's not clear whether Rogers is trying to convince Brock or himself. "She used to say, 'The only way to keep a secret is to tell no one.' "

"Right," says Brock, not at all convinced. He looks Rogers in the eye. "So where is she?"

Rogers does not know.

"Was she upset about anything?" Brock asks.

Rogers is evasive. "Not that I could tell." Rogers stirs his coffee with a spoon. He sips awkwardly. "Well, she was a little unhappy about not going to Paris," he offers.

Now Brock is surprised. "You were going to take her to Paris?"

"We planned a little holiday after the conference." Rogers has been around long enough to know that full disclosure, to his chief aid, is in his interest.

"Not smart" is all Brock says. He knows his job and does it well. A fixer's job isn't to judge, it's to fix.

Rogers sounds like a teenager caught with illicit substances: "She wasn't coming as videographer! And she wouldn't have been travelling under her own name." He is uncomfortable. "I got another passport for her."

This does not look good. Brock wants to know whose passport he planned to use to bring his young lover across the sea with him.

Nothing to do but come clean. "My daughter's. They look similar enough."

"Jesus Christ," Brock says. "Why didn't you let me handle this?"

"Because," says Rogers, "I knew you would have talked me out of it."

"Damn right," says Brock. "This is a fucking disaster."

Rogers' handsome, if slightly disheveled, image is reflected in the mirror on the parlor wall. It does not look like he is going to enjoy the rest of his late-night conversation with Brock.

"How long do you think it's going to take, Senator, for the hysterical mother to hit the airwaves screaming about her lost daughter and the predatory older man who was the last to see her?"

Rogers tells Brock not to worry. He knows Jenny. He can handle her.

"She'll listen to me," says Rogers.

If only he could calm Brock with a pat on the head, the way he patted Connie's head earlier in what is fast becoming a very unpleasant night.

"Don't worry about the mother," he tells Brock again. "*She* isn't our problem."

"Really?" says Brock. "Does she know you're fucking her daughter?"

That little oversight is going to send Rogers back to personal injury law in Broomall, Brock tells the senator. Assuming he doesn't wind up disbarred. Assuming he doesn't wind up in *prison*.

"So what do we do, Bart?" Now *there's* an honest question.

"You wait and pray," says Brock.

"For what?" The senator is genuinely confused.

"If you're lucky, she's turns up dead and soon."

CHAPTER 29

Fanny is gone when Nick wakes up. *Odd*, he thinks. But, honestly, what isn't odd about her? Also, judging by the presence of her bag by the door where Nick left it last night, she will be back. Nick is tired. The couch was not an ideal resting place.

He lumbers into the little kitchen. Though it is French in every conceivable way, it strangely looks much like the mess of a kitchen Nick had in the little Vegas apartment where he enjoyed those fabulous lost days with Elizabeth.

Nick tinkers with the French press coffee contraption, *ooh la la,* pours himself a cup and takes it outside on the little balcony that's connected to his room. *Tres Français.* And *Vive la France* too because it is a lovely day and a good one, as most are, to have a balcony that overlooks a plaza full of very thin women and nondescript but somehow obviously European men. He checks his phone for any messages. He sees the set call is for 8AM.

Nick sips the coffee and eyes a blonde in the plaza. She's willowy and tall. She reminds him of Elizabeth. The pang comes fast in his gut. Elizabeth. Elizabeth. He looks away.

Just to her right, there's the girl from last night taking a big swallow from a cup of coffee and flipping the pages of a copy of the *International Herald Tribune*. She has the look of an American in Paris: rumpled jacket, no lipstick. She's finger-combed her hair.

She smiles up at Nick. Nick smiles back and whips out his iPhone to snap a quick picture. *What's the ending here?* he wonders.

Nick's phone vibrates. He looks at the display and steps inside. It's Manny, his agent.

"Hey, Nick," says the agent.

"Hi, Manny," says the client.

Manny says he just wants to let Nick know that the producer is very happy with his pictures.

"Any word on my book proposal?" That's what Nick wants to know.

"Sorry, pal. Not a peep."

"I bet they didn't even read it," says Nick.

"The title doesn't help." Manny has been harping on this for weeks and Nick is genuinely perplexed.

"What's wrong with the title?"

"*Happy Endings*?"

"Yeah. *Happy Endings*," says Nick.

"Apart from the fact it makes people think of handjobs," says Manny, "what is it that's so happy about your ending?"

"My pictures will tell the story," says Nick.

"Whatever you say, kid," says Manny. "All I can tell you is, it doesn't grab me. Or the publishers."

Nick digs in his heels. Literally. He digs Stan Smith heels into the 19th-century French hotel floor.

"It's a good proposal. Get them to look at it."

"Okey dokey, kid. You're a visionary," says Manny. "Oops. Got another call. Talk to you later."

Nick returns to the balcony. No spring in his step. The girl is smiling at the bright blue sky.

He takes another picture of her.

Could she be his story? There's no love vibe. But there's something about her...

Nick finishes his coffee and deposits the empty cup in the sink, then heads out to the plaza.

¤

Fanny sees Nick approach. She takes the *Tribune* off the seat beside her so he can sit down.

"Feeling better?" says Nick.

"Yeah. Thank you for last night," says Fanny. "I think I had a little bit too much to drink on the plane." *And a lot too much off it.*

Nick extends a hand towards her. "Nick Sculley."

She takes it. "Fanny Cours." She looks around the plaza. "This is very beautiful. You're lucky to get to stay here."

"Just for a little while longer," he says. He tells Fanny about his movie gig. It pays enough, he says. While he waits for his book proposal to gel.

Fanny's thinking that it's nice to be in Paris and not be blotto drunk. Nice to not have to face her mom and tell her about Lee Rogers. (Though she knows she should give her a call. She will. When she's ready.) Also nice not to think about how she might go about confronting Lee now that she's in Paris. There are so many things to not think about, in fact, that she's relieved to be able to focus on Nick for the moment. "What's your book going to be about?"

What is the book going to be about? "It's about a relationship between a man and a woman," Nick says. "How it begins, where it goes, and how it ends."

And just like that, Lee Rogers is back in her mind. "Who's the man?" asks Fanny.

"The photographer," Nick says.

"And the woman?"

For the first time since Nick saw her crumpled up on the train, there's a vaguely flirtatious tone in Nick's voice.

"I don't know yet."

CHAPTER 30

Lee Rogers is concerned. You would be concerned too if the young intern you were sleeping with had disappeared and her hysterical mother were sitting across from you in your living room.

"I've done some checking," Rogers tells Jenny Cours. "Fanny left her apartment two nights ago and hasn't returned."

Lee Rogers deploys his best *everything-is-in-order* voice. Jenny Cours isn't buying it.

"I know that. I called her roommate fifteen times," she says. Jenny wants real help. Not pabulum.

Rogers stirs his coffee. Maybe Jenny and her hysteria will dissolve like the sugar in his cup.

"Did Fanny have a boyfriend?"

Jenny shakes her head. Not a proper boyfriend—Fanny never mentioned anybody special.

Rogers is relieved, on many fronts.

He is relieved, for example, that Connie had a doctor's appointment and returned to Philadelphia yesterday morning, before Jenny called to say she needed to see Lee right away. She was on her way to D.C. on a late-afternoon flight, she said, could they meet in the early evening?

Lee felt a familiar excitement in the face of Jenny's urgency and forgot, just for a moment, that Jenny was calling about Fanny. And, of course, that he might have a real problem on his hands.

"Did she say anything to her roommate?" Lee asks.

Jenny says no, Amy told her that Fanny was gone a few nights a week and so was obviously seeing someone but Amy didn't know who.

"Well! I'll put one of my staffers on it—"

"No, Lee," says Jenny, "this isn't working." She gets up, takes her bag from the table. "I'm going to the police."

Rogers does not need a bunch of police officers poking around looking for his lost intern right now. Or ever.

"No, Jenny. It's premature," he says.

"What are you talking about? My daughter is gone. The only reason I haven't called the police already is that you said you would help."

Rogers senses disaster. "I'm trying to help," he says.

"How? Lee, we need a full investigation. Police. FBI. Whatever it takes. And we need it now."

Rogers suggests that a little discretion might be a good idea.

"Discretion!" Jenny feels like she is having a terrible nightmare. "What are you talking about, Lee? I have nothing to hide. Fanny has nothing to hide. Do you, Lee? Do you have something to hide here?"

Jenny looks around the M Street house. At last, she thinks she gets it. "Look, Lee, I'm sure I'm not the first or last stewardess you bedded in this house. You can count on me not to blab about it on TV. And I'm sorry I can't be worried about other women out there. If stories about your philandering come out in connection with an investigation into your intern, well that's something you'll have to deal with."

"There aren't other women," Rogers tells Jenny. "And there never were."

"Oh please, Lee, I know you," Jenny says. She is impatient. This is an odd conversation to be having at this particular moment.

"No, Jenny, you don't. You never gave me a chance. You just disappeared."

"Disappeared? I was in love with you, Lee. I knew you weren't going to leave your wife. Somebody was going to get hurt. It looked like it was going to be me. I had to break it off."

"Hurt? You weren't hurt too long. You were married within a month. That Canadian pilot. Sure happened fast."

Jenny is drawn into an argument she can't quite believe is taking place so many years after the fact.

"I wanted a husband. And a family. Something that was never going to happen with us. Gene was always there for me. He was a great dad to Fanny."

Rogers stands up, crosses over to the couch, and sits down beside Jenny. He takes her hand and looks deep into her eyes.

"Jenny," he says, "you were wrong about me. I would have left Connie. I loved you so…"

This is madness, Jenny thinks. She pulls away. "Will you stop it, Lee! You're just sweet-talking me out of going to the police. Enough!"

Rogers repeats that it is too soon to involve police.

"Lee," says Jenny as if she's turned suddenly to stone, "do you know something I don't know?"

Rogers shakes his head no.

"No idea who she was seeing?"

He glances away. "I don't keep track of my interns and their social lives."

A terrible realization takes shape in Jenny's mind.

"Oh. My. God. Lee! You didn't…"

Rogers knows what's coming. He is prepared. He answers the question with a well-rehearsed, innocent expression. "Didn't what?" he says.

"Have…Fanny…up here?" The words crawl out, slowly, forfending the answer.

Rogers breaks out laughing. "Oh god, no," he says, bemused innocence on full blast. "How could you even ask that, Jen Jen.

I gave the kid a job so I could have a connection to *you*. Now, please, will you stop with all this?"

Jenny welcomes the reassurance she was looking for. She forces herself back on track. "No, Lee, I won't stop any of this. Until we find her."

Rogers tells Jenny she is looking in the wrong place.

Jenny bursts into tears. "I don't know where to look!"

Rogers reaches for her and takes her in his arms. He attempts to quiet her uncontrollable sobs and succeeds, only partially. The rapid back-and-forth between composure and tears and fury is enervating. Jenny is moving in twenty emotional directions at once. She steels herself now and says, "Lee, you have to know something. Fanny is not just my daughter…she's *our* daughter."

Rogers releases Jenny from his arms. He tries to process what she's just said. "That can't be," he says. "That can't be."

It cannot be, he thinks. Jenny has gone over the edge. Madness.

"No way," he tells her. "We were careful when we were together. I was."

Jenny shakes her head. Her blood thumps madly in her chest. "Not always," she says.

"Jenny—"

"I never told you, Lee. I thought about it, I almost did, I came here…but you were so awful to me that day, and I realized you would want me to end the pregnancy, which…I couldn't. I just couldn't. So I did what had to be done. I broke things off with you and married Gene."

Maybe now that Rogers knows the truth, he'll actually help.

Rogers glances at a photograph of Deron and Tippy, the retriever pup he got for his twelfth birthday.

"Fanny isn't my child," says Rogers. "It isn't true."

He thinks, *It can't be. Because that would be too awful.*

"Yes," says Jenny, "she is. It is true. I married Gene to protect

my baby. He never knew who Fanny's real father was. And neither did Fanny."

On hearing herself say her daughter's name, Jenny bursts
again into tears. "None of it matters now," she says and she
drops to the floor sobbing. The emotional storm and remaining
questions about Fanny—where *is* she?—are too much.

Lee kneels on the floor beside her. "We are going to find
her," he says. "But falling apart isn't going to help. Have you
gotten any sleep?"

Jenny shakes her head. Rogers is in control again. Or he is
trying hard to look that way.

"I want you to go upstairs and lie down. I'm going to make
some calls. Then we'll go to the police together." He kisses her
softly on the forehead.

Jenny is relieved—and also exhausted and exploding with
worry about her daughter. She gets up, smiles gratefully at
Rogers, and walks towards the stairs.

CHAPTER 31

Not much has changed in the guest room during the twenty years since Jenny was last here. The big bed still faces an antique English bureau. And hanging above the headboard is the same gilt-framed mirror that reflected Jenny's tear-stained face so many years ago.

Jenny is not the only woman who vividly remembers what she was wearing during important events in her life. A blue-and-white seersucker shirtdress, white seed pearls, sandals.

The dress had a little red belt that tied in the front. Jenny remembers the precise feeling of pulling the belt around her, around the slight swelling in her belly, and being flush with excitement thinking that Lee's baby was there underneath the belt, underneath her skin, inside her.

Would Lee notice? Probably not.

Women worry endlessly about bulges and minor weight gain. Men never notice. It's not cluelessness exactly and certainly not disinterest.

The animal center: the point where lost and found are the same general idea. That's what men think about. And it's usually a couple of worlds apart from little bumps or bulges on the periphery.

Jenny rang Lee's bell on an August Sunday, all those years ago, fresh from the flight in from the coast. Connie was away, at some dressage meet or something with Deron or Willa. Or was she in Maryland arranging a re-election tea?

Jenny had never registered Connie's whereabouts precisely. Rather she'd kept track in the same way men regard the barely detectable bumps and swells on a woman's form—dressage, tea, whatever, the important thing was Connie was not around today. And if all went well, as Jenny thought it would, Connie would remain far away.

"Jen Jen! My love. You're looking gorgeous."

"Hello, darling." Jenny melted into Rogers' embrace.

"I didn't think you were coming back," he said. "The last time you left... It felt so final."

"Things change," she said.

He pulled her inside. Washington was hardly squeamish about adulterous liaisons. But it was not something Rogers wanted to parade around on his front doorstep.

He picked her up in his arms and walked towards the bedroom.

Jenny held the Congressman's face in her hands, tasted him gently. It was as if no time had passed since the dinner with the napkin and the regretful kiss goodbye. "God, I missed you, Lee."

"Me too."

"I'm hardly alive when we're so far apart."

"Yes, my love. It's the same for me."

They fell onto the bed together. Rogers smothered her with kisses.

They were flush in love. But there was something on Jenny's mind. Should she tell him in bed? Or afterwards, in the kitchen, maybe.

Jenny had thought about this a lot, imagined the scene many times. "Lee, I'm going to have your baby." She would look him in the eye and say the words softly.

In one scene Jenny had imagined, Lee did a quick double take and then burst into a big smile, and took her in her arms and kissed her passionately and rubbed his hands across her belly and told her what deep down she'd always known: that he had never loved anyone like her, he'd never thought he could have everything—brains and beauty and sexy and sweet and light and hot—in one package. And now there would be three!

And in her imagination he picked her up and carried her to the bed and called out to Capitol Liquor to order Dom Perignon— no, on a Sunday Capitol wouldn't be open, so let's say he skipped downstairs and returned with a bottle and poured two glasses and raised a toast, "To my love and my baby love. I love her, and him or her, to death and forever."

Jenny sometimes got carried away.

She'd also imagined cooler, more sober versions of the scene. "My love," Lee murmured, overcome. "My love." He shook his head, wrestling with the pain it would cause Connie when he told her the truth, when he told her he was leaving. But painful as it would be, it had to be done—their baby was paramount and if his marriage and his career had to be sacrificed, so be it.

But that was all imagination, and now Jenny was jolted out of her reverie.

"Honey, are you there? I'm having a little trouble with this belt." Rogers was fumbling at her midsection, utterly oblivious to anything he might have felt beneath the fabric.

"Sorry, darling." Jenny unhooked the red belt and Rogers slipped his hand between her legs.

Jenny sighed. "Oh, darling. We're so perfect together and now…"

Rogers pushed her legs apart and moved on top of her.

Before she could finish her sentence, he'd pulled her panties to one side and pushed himself inside her.

As she remembers it, he came almost immediately, giving out a satisfied gasp of pleasure.

"That was great, honey," he said. He rolled off her and sat up.

"For me too," Jenny lied.

Rogers apologized for being so distracted. He said he was

worried about the primary. He needed to raise more money for ads he wanted to air before the showdown. "Connie has done a hell of a job organizing fundraisers but the money's not coming in fast enough. I'm sorry to bring all this up, it's just...I just can't get it out of my mind. And now I've spoiled our special Sunday."

"I guess it's not the right time..." Jenny said.

"The right time for what?"

"Nothing. You have so much on your mind."

"I always have time for you," he said, glancing at his watch and then adjusting the knot of his necktie.

"Time to fuck me!" Jenny jumped out of bed and started rebuttoning the shirtdress, which had come undone under his groping hand.

"Honey, what's the matter? That's a terrible thing to say."

"Is it, Lee? Have I ever been more to you than a good quick lay?" Jenny felt prompted by something hard, insistent, something good manners couldn't quiet.

"That's not fair, Jen Jen. You know how I feel about you."

"I know how you feel about me in bed. But you know, Lee, that may not be enough for me."

"What's got you so mad?" Rogers asked. "I thought you wanted to..."

"I guess I pictured it going differently." Jenny had her dress buttoned. Her pearls hung crooked.

"How?"

"I don't know, maybe you'd take your time—"

"I was excited," Rogers said.

"Clearly," Jenny said. Then, surprising herself, "You didn't even use a condom. Suppose I got pregnant? Then what?" This is not what she wanted to say. Or at least this is not how she wanted to say it.

Rogers went cold. "That's impossible. I've had a vasectomy."
Jenny was looking for reassurance, not medical updates.

And she had read something about how vasectomies don't always work. But this was not the conversation she'd wanted to have with Lee. Not at all. She felt possessed. Mad. Maybe it was hormonal, baby-driven fury.

"You don't want a woman, you just want a pet to play with." Jenny knelt down on the floor before Rogers and put her hands up in a bizarre mime, pretended to be a dog begging for a treat. "Woof. Woof."

"Get up," said Lee. "Stop that."

Rogers pulled Jenny to her feet. He looked like was poised to slap her on the face. But he restrained himself. He balled his rage into a fist and smashed it not into Jenny as he would have liked but into the wall behind her. Jenny burst into tears and raced into the bathroom, slamming the door behind her.

Jenny remembers all this now, remembers it as clearly as if it had happened moments rather than two decades ago. The face she sees reflected in the guest-room mirror looks exhausted. She turns from her reflection and walks, crying, into the bathroom.

Downstairs, Senator Rogers, visibly shaken, dials the phone.

A few seconds pass, the time it takes a phone to ring twice. Then Rogers says into the phone, "Brock, we've got a problem."

CHAPTER 32

For Jenny, the problem is just beginning. Her face is wet with tears. She sees her reflection in the glass. She is a mess, a sad mess. And Fanny is gone.

Jenny rinses her face with cold water and pats her face dry. She mops back the fresh tears and suddenly she's overtaken by something familiar, very familiar, scary familiar, perfume— Déjà Vu! Fanny's perfume!

Jenny drops the towel like it is on fire. She throws her head back and shrieks.

It's a glass-shattering shriek, the audible sound of a human heart cracking into pieces.

NO NO NO

Fanny has been in this bathroom, dashed her wetness on a towel right here.

NO NO NO

Jenny tries to shout the irrefutable fact out of existence: *NO NO NO NO NO—*

There is nowhere to go but down. And that's where Jenny falls, straight to the bathroom floor, smashing her head on the porcelain sink basin as she drops.

CHAPTER 33

Fanny is enjoying her Paris adventure but she's not quite sure when it should end. Shouldn't she be getting back to work? What work? After that disastrous scene with Rogers, does she still have a job?

Nick's been a doll. Let her crash on his couch, hang out on the movie set. She's watched him take pictures of the actors—and of her. Is she the girl in his book? Fanny told him she's in a relationship, sort of, but Nick keeps shooting pictures of her anyway.

"Why?" she asks while they share a late-night bottle of wine.

Nick scratches his chin. "I don't know. I like the way you look," he replies.

"But I thought your book was about a relationship. We don't have a relationship."

Nick smiles, lifts the camera he always has around, snaps a picture of her looking dubious.

"What are you talking about? We have the best kind of relationship. No sex. No romance. We just enjoy each other's company. Do you have a problem with that?"

Fanny has no problem with that. If Rogers weren't in the picture who knows what might have developed between her and Nick.

"So what are you doing in Paris anyway?" Nick asks.

She's explained about the internship, the webisodes. "The campaign trail got pretty intense. I decided I needed a break."

Nick cocks his head. "Really?"

Fanny nods.

"Wasn't because your webisodes got you into trouble."

"Why do you say that?"

"The camera is a come-on. People instinctively flirt with it."

"Really? That never occurred to me."

But of course it did. Fanny isn't about to tell Nick everything. Mum's the word on her relationship with Rogers. For now.

"He got a hell of a lot more traffic because of me," Fanny says. "That didn't make his campaign manager any happier. What a jerk! I was only there to help."

Nick snaps another picture.

"What was that one for?"

"You're pretty when you're jealous. You get this look in your eye."

"Jealous? Jealous of what?" Fanny protests.

"You and the campaign manager. Fighting for the attention of the sainted candidate. I guess you won—and got the boot."

"I guess."

Nick sees that Fanny is clamming up and shifts gears.

"Look, I've got the same problem on the set. Hildy wants to crawl all over me. But I resist. Not that I would mind a little roll in the hay for old time's sake. But I don't need the jealousy. Both the director and her costar want to fuck her. But she only has eyes for me. God knows why. Scratch that. I know why. She's remembering all that hot sex we had in college. Somehow those first sexual experiences trump all. But what she doesn't remember is what a self-involved bitch she was. One night we decided to go to a motel. We couldn't get any privacy in the dorm. I was on top of her, fucking her brains out, I thought, when she kept on yelling more, more, more. I open my eyes and saw she wasn't looking at me. She was looking at her reflection in the mirror over the bed. She was basically fucking herself."

"I've never experienced *anything* like that."

"While you were pointing your camera at Rogers, didn't you flirt with him a little bit? Look at you, you're a living example of the Heisenberg principle."

"The what?"

"Heisenberg principle. In weighing something your presence is tipping the scale. You're the antithesis of the fly on the wall."

"Well I should hope so. Who wants to be a fly on the wall? I was there to draw him out. Show to the world the true Senator Rogers. Like coaxing a pearl out of an oyster."

Nick's not buying this.

"You have to kill the oyster to get the pearl. Did you?"

Fanny leans back in her chair and remembers when they crossed the line. It seemed so right at the time. So natural. Isn't making love the ultimate communication between a man and woman? Tears start to form in her eyes. She looks back up at Nick. He's aiming the camera at her. And snaps another picture.

"A euro for your thoughts?"

Fanny shakes her head.

Nick puts the camera down.

He reaches across the table and takes Fanny's hand.

And holds it until she stops crying.

CHAPTER 34

Connie is worried. What has gotten into her?

Is it the illness, the medication? She doesn't think so. Yes, she's thin and tires easily. And certain things—walking for a long time, climbing steps—take more effort than before. But really that's not it.

Aging is not an entirely pleasant affair. One day Connie was the beautiful Bryn Mawr graduate. The whole world was open in new ways. Doctor, lawyer, Indian chief. Connie had choices her mother never did. Bryn Mawr pushed hard for certain career choices. Connie's roommates were both going to medical school.

But medicine was not a viable option: Connie didn't give a hoot about radiology or endoskeletal whatevers. Numbers weren't Connie's strength, so banking made no sense. Anyway, her father had money, so work wasn't an issue.

Frankly all Connie really wanted was to get married. She could raise children—and maybe horses—and read great books and have a garden and make wonderful meals and plan nice vacations.

And oh, she'd love her husband, ambitious, fierce-minded, fair, strong, successful. She'd care for a fabulous house, assemble it in good taste, and have nice parties and interesting friends (from good families). Connie couldn't tell anyone any of this. It would be too embarrassing.

That pretty much left law school as the sole viable option.

Columbia was a bit of a shock when she first arrived. But Connie stuck to her dorm, outlined her cases and generally applied herself. She met Lee in her second year and paid far less attention to torts and contracts after she did.

"Bring your lunch and meet me by the river. The 114th Street entrance. At Riverside Drive. You'll recognize me. I'll be looking for you." That's what the note in Connie's book bag said. She found it there one morning after criminal law class ended. Connie remembers the note vividly, each syllable.

Professor Simon had called on the handsome dark-haired man next to her. "Mr. Rogers, can you tell us please, what is the issue in Brady v. Maryland?" Mr. Rogers had exactly no idea. "Professor Simon," he said, "I have exactly no idea what the issue is in Brady v. Maryland."

No one had had the guts to say anything like that before. The class cheered. Lee Rogers came as close as a person could come to taking a bow without actually moving.

Unimpressed, Professor Simon called on Connie Salzman, who quite matter-of-factly delivered the perfect analysis of the Brady rule of exculpatory evidence case. Of course she knew the issue. She'd spent the weekend in her room studying, going through the cases over and over until they practically extruded through her skin.

Connie brought her lunch (a frisée salad) to the river with some trepidation. Who was this smooth-talking Lee Rogers and why did he want to have lunch with her?

Rogers, who'd brought a hot dog for his lunch, spread mustard over the bun with his finger. He produced a blue-and-white bag with the Columbia mascot (a lion) on it.

"Roar," he said, pulling out a bottle of sparkling pink champagne. "Matches the sunset. And your smile."

He pulled two plastic champagne cups from the bag and started to pour.

"First things first," he said, and took a bite of his frank. "Yum." Connie smiled. She was charmed.

But she couldn't help herself. "Do you know what's in those?"

"Whatever it is, it sure tastes good." Lee smiled.

"Have you ever visited a hot dog factory?"

Rogers' eyes twinkled. "Was that on the college tour? I didn't pay much attention after Butler Library."

Connie loved it that he was playful. She giggled—something about him brought out the coquette in her.

"They mix pork trimmings with pink slurry. That's what you get when you squeeze chicken carcasses through metal graders and blast them with water."

Admittedly, Connie's idea of coquettishness was a little odd. She hadn't had much practice. But Rogers was not put off. "How about the bun?" he said.

Connie liked the way he teased. "This is before the bun! Listen. They mix the mush with powdered gunk—preservatives, flavorings, red coloring all drenched in water and then squeeze it through the pink plastic tubes where they cook and package them."

"Now the bun?"

For the life of her, Connie couldn't figure out why she was talking about hot dogs. Something about Rogers made her nervous. The talk was like a tic. But he was having fun. And she couldn't help but enjoy herself.

"Right. Now the bun. I don't think you're taking this very seriously."

"I'm very serious about my hot dogs. Also I'm serious about you, Miss Brady v. Maryland. You look very delicious yourself."

He said this straight out of the blue. Connie blushed.

"Hey! There's some pink slurry flushing across your face."

Connie blushed more. And giggled. What was it about this guy?

Rogers lifted his glass. "To exculpatory evidence." They took a quick sip from their cups. Rogers moved closer. He smelled Connie's sweet (expensive) perfume. "Mmmm. Delicious, yes! And no plastic packaging?"

Connie loved this. So much so, that to her enormous surprise, she heard herself say, "Only one way to find out."

"And what would that be?"

Connie lightly brushed her lips against his. "Any sign of plastic packaging?" she said.

"Nope!" said Rogers. He kissed her again shyly. "What do you think? Will I survive that hot dog and all those toxins?"

"I hope so," said Connie and she did. "Take my breath away," she added. And he did.

A courtship began. Connie helped Rogers outline his cases and prepare for exams. He took her to jazz concerts at divey bars downtown. She got all As. He got offers from the top firms.

Rogers clinched matters when he took Connie to Paris right after graduation (she graduated third in her class; he didn't rank) and proposed to her.

He did not want to be without this fine-looking, straight-thinking woman. He needed her. He loved her too. There was no question: Connie would be the perfect wife.

Connie was over the moon.

You probably want to know what the sex was like then. I'm sorry, Connie Salzman was not the type of girl who talked about things like that. She liked Lee Rogers. A lot. Let's leave it at that. He made her laugh. She did things with him she couldn't imagine.

They were married six months later. Lee had a job at a big Philadelphia firm. Connie had a job at a bigger Philadelphia firm. The job was not interesting. Even slightly.

Connie did not have to worry much about any of this for long. Two months after she started work, she discovered to her delight—true, actual and complete delight—that she was pregnant. The trouble with Lee might have started around this time.

Connie was dizzy with happiness about the pregnancy and

might have lost track. Dinner might have slipped; Connie absolutely did not plan the spring trip to the Alps that year. That she remembers. Lee went instead with a bachelor friend from his firm.

Connie would never have found out about the stewardess he met on the flight. She wasn't a suspicious spouse or anything like that. But she phoned Lee in the Alps—the connection was bad and she thought she'd misheard the hotel operator; she asked for Mr. Rogers and the operator said, in thickly accented English, "I em so sorry, Ma'am. Meester and Meesus Rogers just check out now."

Connie actually said, "No. Not Mr. and Mrs. Rogers. I'm looking for Mr. Rogers. I *am* Mrs. Rogers!"

"I em so very sorry," said the voice on the phone. "So very sorry."

Connie was actually confused and wondering why on earth the operator was so very sorry when the awful truth dawned on her.

Lee's homecoming was not so pleasant as previous ones. Connie did not pick him up at the airport, but was instead waiting for him when he got home.

"Lee. We have to talk," she said.

Rogers had never seen such a stern look on Connie's face. Pregnancy, he thought, makes animals of all of us.

"Who were you with in the Alps? I know you weren't alone. I know you were with a woman. Lee. What. Are. You. Doing?"

Lee Rogers was on his knees so quickly Connie thought he'd had a heart attack. It took him just a few tearful moments to tell her, choking back tears, that yes, he was with a stewardess, someone he'd met on the plane.

He was scared of being a father, he said. Just scared in a way he'd never been before. "I lost my mind, Connie. I was so afraid. I wanted to be a man for you, a strong man who wasn't afraid, and

I wanted to be a strong father for our baby, and Connie, Connie, Connie," he choked back more tears, "can you forgive me? Ever? Oh god, Connie! Please help me to be worthy of you—your love, our baby."

This could've been the end of all that Connie had ever dreamt. She wasn't going to let it slip quickly out of hand.

Determined to save herself, her baby, and the family she dreamt of, Connie got in the car and drove to Bucks County, to the small country house her father had given her and Lee for a wedding present.

Connie had planted a little garden there and it was there that she would find the peace she needed to survive this glitch on the long road she knew would lead to a happy ending for her, for Lee, and for their unborn child.

It was high spring. Connie knew just what she'd do. She'd plant a cherry tree like the ones that had just blossomed in the capital. Sweet, pink and fragrant, the trees represented all of nature's promise.

Trees with sour fruit last longer—up to two hundred years. As a statement about her conviction and the promise of this pregnancy, Connie chose one of these.

She loaded the sapling into her car, ferried it to Bucks County and planted it before she even went inside the house.

Twenty years later, worried about herself and her odd behavior, Connie drives the familiar road to Hillside Lane. There, in front of the house, the first thing she sees is the cherry tree she planted all those years ago.

Now fully mature, it blossoms magnificently over the drive. For Connie the tree is a horrible sight. Each bright pink bloom is a reminder of that time, of what happened with the stewardess.

What happened happened—a long time ago. And then it was over. Lee said it was.

And it was.

And it was awful and unspeakable to have accused him again, to have impugned his integrity with her crass inquiry about the video girl.

It was weak to have questioned him. Rogers made a promise all those years ago: if Connie could forgive him—and she could, she did—never again would he violate their vows or give her cause to worry, ever. A simple exchange: absolution for fidelity, forever.

And she had sunk to questioning his veracity, his honesty. She had violated their trust.

She goes to the shed. On a neat pegboard hang all the tools you'd need to build a new world—hammers, drills, saws. Connie surveys the tools and, at last, sees the hatchet she is looking for.

She picks it up. Weaving just a little, she carries the hatchet to the front of the house and plants her Size 5 feet onto the earth and then she takes a wild swing—not one, in fact, but six— and she does not stop then but continues to hack, chop chop chop, at the twenty-year-old tree that bears with its fruit the bitter memory of Lee's twenty-year-old sin.

The tree falls. The crash is loud. Connie is satisfied. Gone is the tree that memorializes Lee's one and only transgression. She will not question him again. She goes inside and dials her husband's cell. "Lee, I cannot tell a lie. I chopped down the cherry tree." He has no idea what she's talking about.

"I know you kept your promise to me, Lee. After what happened twenty years ago. I know you did, and I do not want any living reminder of the one, twenty-year-old breach in our lives together. I cut down that tree."

Lee laughs. "Darling, you are so silly. Don't be a nut. I've got to go. Committee meeting prep. See you for dinner tomorrow."

CHAPTER 35

The doorbell at the service entrance to Rogers' Georgetown townhouse rings.

Lee Rogers, in casual gear—khakis and polo—answers. He is surprised to find a very large man, wearing black clothes—turtleneck, trousers, parka, all solid black—standing on the step.

Dark shades sit on the man's nose. And his shaven head, stark in the D.C. twilight, adds an extra ominous cast.

"Yes, what can I do for you?" Rogers might as well be welcoming a witness who has come to testify at the Committee on Foreign Relations. He knows his lines. He knows statesmanlike manners.

The man extends a hand. One that is sheathed in a black leather glove. Odd since it's not cold out.

"Where is she?" says the voice attached to the hand.

Rogers finds the question jarring, partly because the man's lips don't move, but also because he recognizes the voice.

"Brock? What is all this?"

"What do you see, Lee?"

"A big guy. Wearing a lot of black clothing. With a strange, grizzled-up face. Brock, what the fuck are you doing?"

Rogers looks at Brock. Jesus Christ, he's wearing a mask! Some sort of rubber thing, the kind you pull over your whole head, like on Halloween. In the half-light it looks almost real.

"Right," Brock says. "A big guy in black clothing—with an unrecognizable face. Guess what will show up on the Neighborhood Association's surveillance tapes. You got it: An unidentifiable man. I don't know, Lee. Maybe you want to carry her out yourself."

Rogers shakes his head.

Brock walks through the townhouse door.

"She told me Fanny is my daughter." Lee wants his fix-it man to fix this one. Fast.

Brock is not impressed.

"There's one thing I know about you, Lee. You make mistakes. But that is one mistake you don't make, in bed. She probably made that up to guilt you into finding her kid. Who, incidentally, I discovered is queen of the one-night stands."

Brock would quite literally say anything so long as it advances his chief task, which is to keep the senator on track.

Not only did Brock not hear anything about Fanny, he knows absolutely nothing about her or her one- (or any-) night stands. Brock himself has not gotten laid in months, and the very words "one," "night," and "stand" make him dizzy.

Maybe the faux report on Fanny will counteract whatever bogus bit about paternity her mom dropped on the senator to guilt him into caring about the lost intern. That's all Brock is thinking.

"Where is she?" he says. Back to being all-business.

Rogers leads his associate upstairs, to the guest bathroom.

Jenny is on the floor, her handbag spilled open beside her. Her eyes are glazed. There's a slight split of skin on her forehead where she hit the basin and where, in the fullness of time, there will likely be a bruise.

Brock takes out a penlight. "She's out. Looks like a stroke. Probably a cerebral embolism." He wouldn't know a cerebral embolism from a barrel of horseshoes. But speaking with confidence has gotten him through tougher spots in the past.

Rogers feels as if he is in a very bad dream. "She'll be alright?" he says.

Brock pretends to feel for her pulse. "Her vitals are strong.

But it looks like she's out cold, maybe in a coma. For now. Let's get her out of here."

He returns to the bedroom, grabs the blanket off the bed. On his way back to the bathroom, glitter catches his eye. On close inspection, Brock sees that it is neither an earring nor a stray jewel but a sliver of glass, coated crimson in one corner. Blood?

Brock picks up the shard and shows it to Rogers. "What's this?"

Rogers studies it for a moment. He's distracted. You would be too if you were talking to someone who was about to carry a live body out of your house in a blanket.

"When Fanny was here, she cut her foot, I don't know, Brock. Let's wrap this up." (Funny how the mind puns even in the most somber moments.)

"Yeah, yeah, could you get me a plastic bag or an empty pill bottle?" says Brock, as he lays the blanket down beside Jenny.

"Why?"

"Just get it."

Rogers, numb and tired, finds it comforting to follow orders. He rummages through the kitchen drawer, finds a Ziploc bag, returns to the guest room, and hands it to Brock. Brock drops the bit of glass into the bag and puts it in his pant pocket. "What are you going to do with that?" says Rogers.

"This is Fanny's blood, right?" says Brock as he finishes rolling Jenny up. She makes a tidy package. Only her feet are sticking out. "You want to know for sure about what the mom told you, I'll get a DNA test." He reaches over to the sink, grabs a Q-tip from a glass jar. "I'm going to need your DNA too. Swab your cheek with this."

Rogers nods, blankly. He has the odd feeling that a *Columbo* episode is unfolding in his house, in his life.

"All right, let's get her out of here," says Brock. He lifts her body from the floor and cradles her weight in his arms. He takes her out through the bedroom and into the hall. One of Jenny's smart air hostess shoes presses against the wall as Brock lugs her down the stairs. Squeak, squeak.

CHAPTER 36

"What are you going to do with her?"

The sight of Jenny, a limp bundle in a blanket, now hanging over Brock's shoulder, makes Rogers queasy.

"You don't want to know. Stay in the dark. What you don't know you don't have to lie about."

Rogers wishes he were a little more numb than he actually is. Connie. Fanny. Jenny. How did everything spin out of control. Brock with Jenny over his shoulder. Really. Rogers doesn't even know where he got on the lunatic road that's brought him here.

Brock carries his burden to the service door. "Let's hope to god she stays out of the picture until we find her fucking daughter. Doesn't the girl have a cell phone?"

"Yes, of course. I keep getting her voicemail."

"Keep trying."

Brock carries Jenny out, stuffs her into the back seat of his car. Where should he leave this package? Brock is used to crisis. But this is a new one even for him.

He is pleased to see, as he heads towards Rock Creek Park, that it is an especially dark evening. He pulls off the road, parks on a deserted dirt path, grabs a thing or two from the trunk, then unwraps the blanket in the back of the car and lifts Jenny out. He holds Jenny in his arms in front of him as if he were carrying her over a threshold. He walks down a deserted path, and lays Jenny on the grass several feet from the path.

Slowly he kneels beside her and, listening to make certain they are entirely alone in the dark, he clamps his hand over her mouth. He fixes her nose in his big palm and shuts it down, tenderly almost, until her breath is gone.

He holds on for an extra minute. Just to make sure.

All done, thinks Brock.

Except of course he's not.

He opens the collapsible shovel he took from his trunk.

The digging is slow, hot, tedious work. Halfway through, the mask he was wearing lies discarded on the ground beside him. The hell with it. No one around to see him now, and if there were, no disguise would help him.

When he's got a Jenny-sized rectangle roughed out—not very deep but it'll have to do—he rolls her into the ground. Then he stands in the dark, shoveling dirt back into the hole. It takes at least ten minutes—lots of dirty, heavy lifting—to put the disturbed earth (and Jenny's bones) to rest.

And Brock's work is still not done. He gets up, walks back to his car, and drives to the DDC.

CHAPTER 37

Rogers is on the sofa in his living room when Brock returns. He's slumped over, and has a dazed *how-did-I-get-here?* expression.

Brock pulls a chair out from the 18th-century English writing desk and sets it down facing Rogers. He grabs him by the shoulders and shakes him hard.

"Pull yourself together."

Brock might as well be on Neptune. Connie. Fanny. Jenny. Rogers doesn't know where to start putting things back in order. Connie is going to kill him. If all this messes up his re-election prospects…

"Senator. We've got work to do. We can get this under control. First, you call a press conference…"

"What about Jenny?"

"Forget her. She didn't make it."

"Oh my god." Rogers looks stricken. "No. No. No. I thought you said—"

"By the time I…deposited her…she was gone."

God, no. Please. God. No. Not a scandal before the election, Rogers thinks. *Connie is weak. This could kill her. No…*

Brock interrupts his panic. "Right now, these are the facts: Distraught mother confronts daughter's seducer and dies." He lets Rogers process this.

Rogers starts to tremble.

"We're going to jail, Lee. Unless…"

Suddenly Rogers is very alert. "Unless?"

"Unless we spin the facts. And we can only do that if Fanny is quiet. *Kept* quiet."

"Kept quiet? Are you crazy? She's a kid. And she could be my kid!"

Brock is stone-faced. "It doesn't matter what she is."

"I have to know," says Rogers.

"Alright, alright." Brock pulls a piece of paper out of his pocket. "DNA test results. Do you want to read it yourself?"

"How did you get that done so quickly?"

"I've got a friend at the DDC lab."

The blood drains from Rogers' face. He pushes the paper away.

"You tell me what it says."

Brock holds the paper up. He pulls back the way middle-aged people do in order to read clearly.

Rogers can't see the paper, which if he could would stop his heart (not to mention his campaign); in clear bold print, the paper says *Paternity Test Results: POSITIVE*.

"It says: *Negative*," Brock says. And he says it with the full conviction of the practiced liar.

Relief floods Rogers' face.

"She made the whole thing up," Brock says. "Just another devilish leopard in the jungle that is public life. It's war, Lee. Politics and jungle life. One big war. And you know what they say, war isn't about who's right, it's about who's left."

Rogers isn't listening anymore. He wonders if it's getting hot inside or what. He pulls his collar away from his skin. It's damp. Everywhere.

CHAPTER 38

Elizabeth, still enjoying the Monhegan quiet, wonders whether Dottie's advice makes any difference to anyone. She tries hard to imagine being so desperate you turn to a faceless newspaper columnist for help. She doesn't think she's ever slipped that low.

There has always been someone there to rescue Elizabeth. Bruce was there when things were really bad, during what Elizabeth remembers as the darkest days of her life. And then Nick. All part of the past now.

She's done a kind of self-cauterizing, closed down the nerves that led to certain memories. It was a kind of suicide; she seared the edges off her mind, her heart and everything else that was once alive and attached to the person she used to be.

There are some (notably those who were left behind) who might find something monstrous about Elizabeth and the way she rubbed out her own past, eliminated it wholesale from her mind. And maybe there is.

Sometimes you're preyed upon, sometimes you're the predator. This is what Elizabeth would have thought if she were capable of or interested in thinking it through, which she isn't.

Call it monstrous. Call it whatever you want. Elizabeth survived.

She remembers arriving in Las Vegas. She was entirely *Elizabeth,* the new Elizabeth, when Bruce picked her up in the Atomic Café where she'd gone to refuel after getting off at the bus station, all that she owned in the world packed into one not-all-that-heavy duffel bag.

"Baby, you're too pretty to eat alone," he said. "Mind if I bring my Meltdown Coffee and Atom Bombe cake over and sit with you?" Bruce was about as easy with the clichés as the Atomic Café menu.

"Sure, why not." Elizabeth gave Bruce a quick once-over. She didn't need to go much farther than the Gucci loafers. It was obvious who Bruce was or wanted to be: a big-money player, a Vegas high-roller, one with all the class money could buy.

The coincidence—the fact that Bruce was in fact the very person Elizabeth was supposed to contact when she arrived in Vegas—soon emerged and cemented what was already inevitable.

Some things aren't complicated. Rich, single guy who fancies himself a collector of treasured objects meets pretty blonde in a café, bombards her with flirtatious remarks and, well, if she's looking for anything (which Elizabeth was, namely a place to live and a new life to go with it), it's not hard to guess that a bed might soon be in the picture.

The idea of being Mrs. Diamond didn't occur to Elizabeth right away. But it didn't take long. The sheets on Bruce's bed were a clincher. They were the crazy softest thing Elizabeth ever felt in her life. Working at fast-food restaurants for fast-food pay didn't exactly bring in money for 1,600-thread-count Egyptian cotton sheets.

The house had a big pool. Elizabeth sat beside it when it wasn't too hot and swam laps when it was. People watching might be hard pressed to find evidence that Elizabeth had a mind. There were no books on the poolside table. No *International Herald Tribune*. But no one would deny that she had a killer body. The 40-50 laps a day didn't hurt. Plus they had the convenient effect of filling a lot of time.

What else did Elizabeth do with her days? She taught herself how to spend money. She'd never had any before. Shoes. She loved shoes and bought herself a whole closet full of Louboutins, Jimmy Choos.

Where was she supposed to wear these? The one magazine she read from time to time was *Vegas Today*, which her husband owned, and in its pages she saw how Nevada's smart set dressed. She also watched the women in Bruce's casinos. She was a quick study and a great mimic.

It didn't take long before she got it: the Choos, replaced by cooler, low-key fare, went unworn after Elizabeth learned that jeans and fancy t-shirts actually gave a good-looking woman a richer, more natural look, and frankly more of a "fuck you" look too.

Throw on some diamond earrings and a tasteful $300,000 Patek Philippe watch and *voila!* Elizabeth fit right in with the expensively maintained supermodels and actresses who sometimes came to town and blew everyone away with their *Who me? I barely gave a thought to my appearance!*

Bruce was okay at first. He bought her things, fucked her hard, left her alone. But it got old fast. And the jealousy that followed gave Elizabeth a big pain.

"Who's that punk hanging around by the pool?" "Why did that guy at the blackjack table give you that look?" "Why are you so giddy after you go to the gallery in the afternoon?" Bruce suspected everyone from the pool man to his accountant. As if.

The more remote Elizabeth got, the more intense Bruce's jealousy. He checked her email. It wasn't like there was a lot to check. Elizabeth's correspondence was limited to a girlfriend or two she'd met at the hotel, "Facial this afternoon?", and receipts from Neiman Marcus and the other stores from which she ordered shoes and dresses and later jeans and t-shirts.

It got annoying. For about five minutes. Then Elizabeth took comfort in the pool man, the accountant, the guy at the gallery.

All the men that Bruce suspected. Okay, not the pool man. Or the accountant. But the art dealer, the guy from Chicago who was in town for the World Series of Poker, the trainer at the gym, the maître d' at the steak joint in the Diamond Casino. Oh, and Nick Sculley the good-looking kid from New York.

CHAPTER 39

Rogers is clean and dry when the doorbell rings thirty-six hours later, but inside? Inside, he's still sweating and has been the whole time. He's just finished reading the papers—the *Washington Post*, *New York Times* and *Wall Street Journal*—and has forced down the fruit and oatmeal sprinkled with flax and chia seeds that Connie, ever mindful of his health, likes him to eat for breakfast.

Connie, thank god, is still in Pennsylvania.

Jenny's body—wherever Brock left it—hasn't been found yet. Or at least if it has been, it's been kept out of the papers.

But here it is, 7AM on a Wednesday morning, and Rogers' doorbell is ringing. A sixth sense tells him it's not unrelated.

Rogers dabs the corners of his mouth, folds his napkin, pushes his chair back from the table, and makes his way with a great show of calmness (performed for no one's benefit but his own) to the front door.

D.C. Detective Emmett Ernst stands at the door holding a leather case that flaps open to reveal his badge.

"Sorry to bother you at home, Senator." Ernst looks genuinely sorry, but as a professional faker of genuineness, Rogers isn't buying it. "I need to ask you a few questions about a woman I believe you know, a Ms., uh, Cours?"

They found her. And now they've found me. Goddamn it, Brock, why aren't you here to get me out of this?

"I do," Rogers says, carefully. "Know her. I did, many years ago."

"Years?" The detective looks puzzled. "I thought she joined your campaign at the end of the summer."

"Oh!" Rogers says, with relief. "You mean Fanny. I thought you meant her mother."

"Well, her mother's part of it," Ernst says. "But I do mean Fanny. Apparently her mother's been unable to locate her. Her roommate says Fanny hasn't been home or reachable for several days."

"And that's a matter for the police? She's a college student. Maybe she decided to take a trip somewhere."

"Maybe so," Ernst says. "But now her mother's unreachable as well. She telephoned her daughter's roommate, Amy, uh—" He pulls a small spiral-bound notepad from his pocket and flips through it. "—Rosenbaum more than one dozen times in a twenty-four-hour period, expressing severe concern about her daughter's not having arrived on a flight home as planned. She insisted that Ms. Rosenbaum call her daily to check in and now she seems to be unreachable herself. Her phone's not answering. So Ms. Rosenbaum called us." The detective looks past Rogers into the entry foyer. "May I come in?"

"Of course." He ushers Ernst into the living room, offers him coffee. Offers him oatmeal with flax and chia seeds. "Keeps you healthy—or so says my wife, ha ha."

Ernst does not want oatmeal or seeds. Nor, for that matter, does he want a bunch of gladhanding chitchat from a slick D.C. insider with a bunch of photos of horses and dogs all over his living room. But he keeps the smile on his face, the tone of deference in his voice.

"So, do you have any idea where Ms. Cours is?"

"The daughter," Rogers says.

"Either of them."

"No. I'm sorry to say I don't. I'd like to help—I really would. But the fact of the matter, Detective, is that I really didn't know the daughter well at all. I just gave her the internship as a favor to an old friend. She joined the campaign to do some videos for school credit, an inside look at how a campaign works on the road, that sort of thing."

"Did she interview you?"

"Once or twice, I think so, I don't really remember. A couple times maybe."

"Where?"

"Where?"

"Where were you when she interviewed you?"

"You mean what towns?"

The detective is shaking his head. "What settings."

"Ah, let me see. Campaign buses, planes, hotel lobbies."

"Were you ever alone with her?"

"Golly, I'm just not sure. Maybe. It's possible, I guess, yes."

"Have you heard from her in the last seventy-two hours?"

"No sir, I haven't. Not for some time."

"How much time?"

"We have eight interns this summer, Detective. Busy kids. Smart too. I don't keep close tabs on them, and I don't remember the when and where of every conversation I have with them. I've got a campaign to run and a lot of other things I need to focus my attention on."

"So you're saying you don't remember when you saw her last?"

"Exactly."

Detective Ernst looks around the room. At the bookcases with their leatherbound books and at the photos—Rogers with Presidents Bush and Carter and Clinton. (Is he really staring into Rogers' eyes in that photo? Yes. It seems that he is. Amazing. Probably remembers Rogers' name too.) Ernst's glance travels down a shelf to a photo of Willa on a horse, and from there down to the parquet floor. He notices something. Something that looks like a faint trace of a stain, a brownish streak. He looks back at Rogers.

"Senator, your security detail told us that Fanny Cours came by to visit you here, last Friday around nine in the evening."

"Oh, yes. Yes. Yes, I remember now, she came here to discuss some plan for her videography. We didn't speak long."

"I understand she was here for some time," Ernst says. "If you didn't speak long, what did you do for the rest of the time?"

It's the most pointed question he's asked yet, but Rogers smiles another of his engaging smiles and answers calmly, confidently.

"I doubt she was here more than twenty minutes. If my people told you otherwise, they were mistaken. They probably just missed seeing her leave."

Detective Ernst squats down next to the stain on the floor. "What happened here?"

"Cut myself," Rogers says. "Thought I wiped that up."

"I'm sure that's right," Detective Ernst says, "and I know this will sound terrible, but would you mind if we test it? Just protocol, you understand. The department'll have my ass if I don't follow procedure."

Poof, the near unctuous grace with which Rogers greeted Ernst finally vanishes and is quickly replaced by chill efficiency.

"You can test anything you want, but you'll have to come back with a warrant first. I mean, if we're talking about following procedure here. And if you have any more questions, I think the proper *protocol* would be for me to have my lawyer present. Good morning, Detective."

Rogers shows Detective Ernst the door.

CHAPTER 40

Has Elizabeth really allowed herself to be rescued by a series of different men? On reflection, she doesn't think so. In fact insofar as she thinks about it at all, she is insistent that the one and only rescuer in Elizabeth's story has been Elizabeth.

She's used what she had, used it to the fullest, and in the direction of not just survival, but triumph. Good sheets. Nice shoes. Well-muscled bodies. And now, a pretty view, a lot of quiet, the song of larks, money in the bank and Dear Dottie letters that are full of marvels and keep her wondering.

What is the matter with "Fighting Hard" and "It Won't Be Long" and the rest of the Dear Dottie gang? Also why are the letter writers almost 100% women? Don't women take more anti-depressant medicine than men? Shouldn't that help? Elizabeth is genuinely puzzled. This does not interfere with the pleasure of the long days on Monhegan Island.

There isn't a lot to do here. Elizabeth has begun to read. Detective novels mostly. She takes long walks. It's a hike to the store where she goes every day to buy groceries. Then she makes herself nice meals which she enjoys by candlelight in the front room of her cottage. Time is a luxury.

Elizabeth looks out at the water. She would like to be more useful to the Dear Dottie gang. How could she do that? She noodles over the question as she walks up the rocky Maine coast.

The last detective novel she read gives her an idea. What if she injected herself into the lives of the Desperate-and-Not-Long-to-Live? Just a little. Or a lot. Maybe she could teach these sad letter writers how to take a little more control of their fate. Or better yet, maybe she could show them.

Dear Dottie,

My husband beats me. I got out of the hospital last week. My husband greeted me with a phone book. He smashed it over my head. This doesn't leave marks. But it sure knocks you out. I'm actually worried my brain is damaged. It's hard to think straight. I'd like to go, but I have two kids and my husband will kill me—or them—if I try to leave. What do I do? I don't have a job and there is little money as is and it all comes from my husband's work as a deliveryman.

Deliver Me Please

Dear Deliver Me Please,

You're still asking good questions, ones like "What should I do?" So your brain's not damaged, yet.

Here's a tip. Call 911. Give them the 411.

Your monster husband should be behind bars.

If that doesn't work, find a pipe.

Show your husband what a good smashing is all about.

Maybe when he's sleeping.

A little self-defense goes a long way.

Legally and otherwise.

I'm rooting for you,
Dottie

Elizabeth is surprisingly sad after she hits the "send" key on this one. It is hard to believe there's a happy ending in store for Deliver Me Please. Or that Dottie's letter has contributed much to it.

Elizabeth's skill at mimicry and self-invention directs a week-long research project. Lots of people have applied themselves to the subject of the perfect murder and how to commit it. It's not hard to find ideas online and Elizabeth has all the time in the world.

The research provides a little light. The letters can be a real downer on sunny afternoons. Even the harmless ones get old fast.

Dear Dottie:

My ex-boyfriend may be coming to visit soon. But I doubt it. In any case, he hasn't let me know. He doesn't initiate contact either, although he responds when I do. I hoped we could have a friendship, but aren't friends supposed to care about one another? Why isn't he curious about me? Can old lovers be friends? I know his circumstances are tough these days, so should I be patient? Am I being selfish or narcissistic in my expectations? Do I even want this friendship?

Signed,
I Wonder

Dear I Wonder,

Yep, your ex-boyfriend may be coming to visit soon. He might arrive on a white horse and shower you with kisses and ride you off into a sunset where he will make passionate love to you until you beg for mercy.

Also, monkeys may fly out of my butt.

Seems just as likely.

In a word, I Wonder, no. You don't want this "friendship." But even if you do want it, it ain't happening.

Dottie

Dear Dottie,

My husband is an abrasive prick. He's a cheat. I found the emails. But then he broke his leg. He couldn't walk. He's the father of my child so I stayed with him and nursed him back to health. As soon as he recovered, he left me for the other woman. How could I be so dumb? Did I get my just desserts?

Dear Just Desserts,
*   Yeah, you are dumb. Get smart.*
*   Better yet, get a hatchet.*
*   Take that bum leg off—and then his head.*
*   Fondly,*
*   Dottie*

Clickety-clack, hit "send." Elizabeth stretches out her long legs. My goodness, she thinks practically every one of these letters is an invitation to murder.

CHAPTER 41

Nick is in bed. He's surfing the web, a little aimlessly. *TMZ*, the *New York Post*, the *Las Vegas Light*.

He's link-hopping through the tabloids when a familiar face flashes past. The face, which is attached to a sexy girl in tight jeans and a sweater, belongs to Fanny.

The headline on the news item says *Rogers Offers Reward for Info About Missing Intern*. The article goes on to explain that she's been missing for a week and that, at a press conference, the senator offered a $10,000 reward for information regarding her whereabouts. She was last seen at his townhouse, but he swears there was no improper or romantic involvement. He just has ordinary concern for a staff member's well-being.

Nick is interested. How could he not be, given that Fanny is in his bathroom at this very moment? He clicks on the story. It comes complete with a quote from Rogers.

"Fanny is a wonderful young lady with so much potential, and we pray she's safe and sound."

Safe and sound. Hmm. That's definitely how Fanny seemed to Nick when he saw her last.

He pulls himself out of bed and marches over to the hotel room's little kitchen. A total mess, of course. He takes down two bowls and a box of Muesli and starts making coffee, for two.

He props his iPad—and the news item about the missing intern—up against the Muesli box. Then he waits.

It doesn't take long before Fanny, wearing the same jeans

she has on in the photo and a blue French-striped cotton top, ambles into the kitchen.

"Hi! What are you up to?" she says. Then she sees the iPad on the table.

She moves closer and reads the item. "Oh my god! My mom must be worried to death. I've got to call her."

The caffeine hasn't yet hit. Nick looks at Fanny skeptically. "Just friends?"

Fanny rummages through her bag looking for her cell phone. "Well…not exactly."

"No one knows you're here?"

"You know."

"No one in your life, though."

Fanny shakes her head. It's half in response to Nick and half because she's found her cell phone and it has no service. Of course not. Why would it, five thousand miles from home? It's a miracle it even has any battery left.

" 'No improper or romantic involvement,' " Nick quotes.

"Well. *I* don't think it's improper," Fanny says. "I think it's the most proper thing in the world."

"You're sleeping with him?"

Fanny nods. "We're in love."

"In love."

"Very much."

She drops the phone back in her purse. It's beginning to dawn on her that the whole Rogers thing has just taken on a whole new life.

"What about his wife?" Nick smells the coffee.

"He said he was going to tell her after the election."

"Then why the vanishing act?"

"Big disaster. First, I'm thrown off the campaign. His manager, this guy Barton Brock, can't stand having me around. Then

Lee planned a trip for us to Paris. Suddenly his wife decides *she* wants to come. I'm dumped again."

Barton Brock. Isn't he the guy in Elizabeth's story, the one who chased her out of town? Elizabeth mentioned something like this to Nick once, after she'd knocked back a few too many.

Barton Brock.

Nick is sure it's the same guy. And now he's playing a similar role in the life of the sloshed kid who wound up sharing Nick's hotel room.

"What are the odds?" That's what Katie Couric said, on national TV, when the second plane hit the World Trade Center on 9/11. What *are* the odds, Katie?

And yet. This character Brock who played a role in his last girlfriend's life turns up pulling the strings in a senatorial campaign involving a guy who's feasting on Miss Fanny Cours.

Nick makes a mental note to hit the web and check out what this Cagliostro looks like.

He reels his thoughts back from the outer banks. A paroxysm of brotherly concern washes over him.

"Listen, kid, let's go sit in the sunshine and have a little chat."

Fanny is game. "Maybe I should call my mom first," she says. But she senses a kind of polite urgency from Nick and doesn't want to slow things up.

Nick knows the ideal café. He orders a double espresso. His French is good. French remains completely beyond Fanny. "Café au lait," she says in perfect English.

The waitress, thin in the astonishing way French women are (meaning that, despite her teensy little waist, she has nice round breasts that go nicely with her perfectly round bottom), brings the coffee. Nick looks pensive.

"Hey, kid, what are you doing with this guy? The senator guy?"

"Look," says Fanny. "I know. I know. It seems crazy. But there's something between us. Not just sex. But something. Something that matters a lot to me. Something I don't think you find every day."

Nick is skeptical. "Maybe," he says.

It really is too bad he doesn't smoke. If he did, this would be a perfect time to inhale.

"The thing is, even if there is something real here, this isn't going to end well."

Nick looks genuinely concerned. And also very attractive.

Fanny protests. But in her heart she knows Nick is right, at least partly.

"I mean, what are you going to do, run off into the sunset or something? And then wake up in the morning as Mr. and Mrs. Senator and film some videos and host a lot of A-list Washington parties? I don't know, Fan, I don't see it."

Nick doesn't get it, Fanny thinks. But he definitely gets something. No, Fanny can't see herself having tea with a bunch of Pamela Harriman types or anything like that. But that doesn't mean that there isn't something real—a sweet hot light connection—between her and Lee Rogers.

"Tell me about you," says Fanny. She wants to change the subject, just for a minute while she thinks things over.

Fanny wants to know Nick's story. Not because she's interested in Nick. She is. Just not in *that* way.

He's definitely appealing. In lots of ways. And it's not like he's trying to smother her or prey on her or anything like that. Fanny could use a big brother. And this guy, in his crisp white shirt with the double espresso, is the closest thing around right now.

"I had a thing with someone who was married too. Didn't end well. Didn't even end."

Fanny doesn't know how to describe the look in Nick's eye. Not dreamy exactly, more like lost.

He looks out into the plaza, past all the people going back and forth to who knows where, past the ice cream sellers and the tourists with their maps, but he doesn't seem to find whatever he's looking for.

"What do you mean it didn't end?"

Nick says, "She was tall and blonde. A real knockout. She had an awful marriage to some rich Vegas guy. Saved her when she was in trouble, rescued her from some bad shit. I loved her right away. Met her on a plane. Ever hear that song with the line 'Love is an angel disguised as lust'? That's what happened here. Real heat melted into real love."

Fanny is interested. She wonders if this is what happened with her and Lee. "Then what happened?" she asks.

"She felt the same way. We were just so together. The marriage made no sense. She couldn't sustain it anymore. There was a dust-up. Nasty. When it was over, she told him the marriage was over too, she was leaving. We drove away in her car. She had this little tiny overnight bag. She said she didn't need anything but me and a t-shirt or two." Nick smiles at the memory.

Fanny gives him a *go on* look.

"We drove to this hotel the husband owned. She went inside to get something, a painting that was worth a lot of money. And…she never came back."

"What do you mean she never came back? Where did she go?"

"No idea. She disappeared."

"Did she go back to her husband?"

"No. I know he looked for her, too. Didn't find her."

"What? How could that be? Were police involved?"

"For a while, I guess. There was a burned-out car at the edge of the desert, they thought she might have died in that—there wasn't a body, but in the desert there wouldn't be, necessarily.

Scavengers. They investigated the husband. He had a motive. But they turned up jack. No trace. Ever."

They turned up jack. No trace. Ever.

Nick is surprised to find he feels slightly nauseous as he tells Fanny his tale. How can someone just disappear like that? Did she have another boyfriend? Or, or, or… Who disappears? Makes no sense.

"Here's a thing I know, Fanny. You're in bed or you're in love with someone and it feels real and solid and it's just you two and the rest of the world melts away, but the thing is the rest of the world *doesn't* melt away. Not really. The angry crazed husband, the campaign manager, they're there, behind the scenes, moving things around in ways you don't see but that change everything, rearrange the basic facts of your own life. That sounds paranoid, maybe, but it's true.

"After the whole thing with Elizabeth, I was kind of lost, as you might imagine. I wanted her. I wanted to find her so badly my body ached for weeks. After a while I just wanted an answer: where was she? The constant wondering was terrible: *Where is she? Where is she? If I don't charge my phone, will I miss her call? If I leave the house will I miss her? Is the husband fucking with me? Does he know where she is? Where the fuck is she?* I'm a photographer, right. So I started taking pictures, places she might be, places we'd been together. And I had a ton of photos of her, of course. I put together a proposal for a book. But I can't find an ending. And shooting pictures didn't stop the questions: *Where is she? Where did she go?* It was driving me nuts.

"After a while, I couldn't take it anymore. I had to get away. Away from the phone that didn't ring, the questions I couldn't answer, the photographs that had no ending."

"So you came here?"

Nick takes a sip of espresso. "Yeah. Took this job as a set photographer and..." He stops himself, returns to Fanny and her tale.

"Listen, kid, if Barton Brock got you kicked off the campaign, you can bet that at this point in what is now a big scandal, he'll want you to keep disappeared."

"What do you mean, 'keep disappeared'?"

"Probably everybody already thinks Rogers was having an affair with you and that's somehow connected with your disappearance, but there's a difference between thinking it and knowing it. What happens if you just turn up? How are you going to explain where you were?"

"I don't know. Tell them the truth?"

"Uh, Fan, I don't think that will get you the senator. But it will end his political career. That's not exactly in your interest, babe."

"I don't *want* it to happen!"

"He doesn't know that."

"When it turns out I'm alive and well, why would the rest of it come out at all? I mean who cares?"

"People care when senators sleep with their staffers."

Hell. Fanny knows he's right. And is it really true that she doesn't want to end Rogers' career? She wants to end his marriage, that's for sure. She wants Lee Rogers to love her more than he loves anyone else. And to act accordingly. That's what she wants.

She honestly doesn't care about the rest, the press, the Senate, whatever.

"I just want him," Fanny says. "That's all I want." And her voice is so plaintive and earnest that Nick swallows his comeback, which would've been, *Well you can't have him.* Is there some way she could? And if so, could this be his story? Instead of boy meets girl, it's girl meets boy—only it's girl meets married senator. Then, of course, girl loses married senator. And the ending is…girl gets married senator? But how?

"He's never going to acknowledge you unless you force him to," Nick says. "He just won't. He's got too much to lose."

"I don't believe that."

Nick raises a hand. "Just hear me out. He's got too much to lose, so he won't take the first step. It's too risky. But if *you* take the first step and cost him his career, he'll hate you for it. So that's no good either. But what if the media does it for you?" He nods towards the camera hanging by its strap from the back of his chair. "You said he was planning a trip to Paris with you, but then he decided he'd bring his wife instead. Okay. So that means he's going to be here soon. Meanwhile, you've been missing for more than a week, the media's been playing it up. They're eager for any news about you. Let's say you're snapped on a sidewalk in Paris. Just before your senator shows up in Paris. I have a friend, a paparazzi, who'll know the right places. You're seen coming out of a building that's known for clandestine assignations. See what I mean?"

"There are entire buildings known for 'clandestine assignations'?" Fanny asks.

"In Paris? There are entire streets."

But Fanny is shaking her head. "I don't accept your premise," she says with the finality of the high school debater she was not so very long ago. "That he won't acknowledge me. He loves me."

Nick swallows his first reaction again. "We'll see," he says.

"Hey," Fanny says, putting a hand on Nick's arm. "I meant to ask, can I use your phone?" He raises an eyebrow. "I really need to call my mom. This whole thing has got to be torture for her."

"Will you tell her where you are?" That would be one way to set his plan in motion. Mom would surely tell someone, and every news bureau covering the missing intern story would instantly direct their attention to Paris.

But she says, "No, just that I'm okay."

He sighs, hands over his iPhone, watches as she enters the number.

They wait.

It rings and rings and rings.

CHAPTER 42

Why should Elizabeth Diamond, aka Dear Dottie, trouble the surface of her very pleasant (if quiet) life to engage in other people's dramas, especially if she amps up the stakes with criminal activity?

The question is on Elizabeth's mind as she peels off her clothes and jumps naked into the ocean. She's gotten used to the temperatures here, and swimming focuses her thoughts.

When she emerges, fifteen minutes later, blood thumping and hot from the exertion in the ice-cold water, she's clear.

First off, she could use a challenge. Surviving is a big deal, yes. But saving someone else's life would count as a real accomplishment. Of a different order than saving yourself.

Second, Elizabeth is pretty sure she can get away with murder. She's thought this through a bit. If Bruce with all his fancy high-paid detectives couldn't find her with her short black hair on Monhegan Island, why would anyone connected with one of the sad souls who write to Dottie think Elizabeth had anything real to do with their lives?

Elizabeth knows that, aside from computer records, one of the main reasons people who try to bump off a spouse get caught is that it's easy to trace the money they pay the killer to do their work: husband is shot under mysterious circumstances; four weeks before, wife withdraws ten grand from her separate checking account. Mistakes like this make detective work easy. Want to get away with a hit job? Keep money out of the picture.

Another thing. Remember the girl who disappeared on the Bahamian island? Very instructive. If you want to bump someone off and get away with it, it's a good idea to do your business in a backwater locale where the police force wouldn't know DNA evidence if it hit them in the head and anyway are too busy comporting with corrupt justice officials to care too much about one dead tourist. Also murder is not great for tourism, so officials in offshore backwater spots hardly want to make a lot of hay out of a killing. They want to bury it quickly and move on.

Elizabeth fixes herself a nice lobster salad, pours herself a glass of wine and heads off to sleep on it.

Up at dawn, she's at the laptop, pulling up the letter Lucy Wideman took out of her bag months ago on the Trailways bus.

CHAPTER 43

Fanny and Nick are in a cyber café. Fanny brightens the screen on her laptop so that she can make out the interview with Rogers that's playing on some network news show.

Brightened, the screen reveals Missy Masters, a hard-news correspondent, and Lee Rogers. Missy is drilling the senator. She fires one question after another. Were they not talking about her, Fanny would definitely switch it off.

"Senator Rogers, do you know what happened to Fanny Cours?"

"No, I do not."

"Did you have anything to do with her disappearance?"

"No, I didn't."

"Did you say anything or do anything that could have caused her to drop out of sight?"

"Fanny and I never had a cross word."

"Do you have any idea if there was anyone who wanted to harm her?"

"I can't imagine there was, no."

"Did you cause anyone to harm her?"

"Good lord, of course not."

"What exactly was your relationship with Miss Cours?"

"She came to work on the campaign, shooting videos for the web. We worked together on those videos." Rogers leaves it at that, but Missy lets the silence stretch on, an old interviewer's trick. Even a veteran interviewee like Rogers finds himself compelled to throw some more words out, to fill the silence. "It's a small campaign, long hours. You become close."

"Close, meaning…?"

"We had a close working relationship. I liked her very much."

"Was it a sexual relationship?"

Rogers shakes his head. "Missy, Connie and I have been married for almost thirty years, and I won't say I'm a…a perfect man, I've made my share of mistakes. But we have a strong marriage. In fact, when I'm in Paris, Connie and I are going to celebrate our thirtieth anniversary by renewing our marriage vows."

The bulldog reporter's expression softens.

"On the top of the Eiffel Tower. October 25, three in the afternoon. That's where I proposed to her thirty years ago."

"Wouldn't our audience love to see that?"

Rogers' clenched jaw relaxes into a smile.

"How is Mrs. Rogers doing?"

"She's getting stronger every day."

"I'm glad to hear that. But can you tell me this—do you think it's possible that Miss Cours was also in love with you?"

"Golly, Missy," Rogers says. His cheek involuntarily twitches. "I don't think so. No."

"Were you in love with her?"

"Absolutely not."

Fanny's face hardens.

She looks at Nick. He looks back, waiting to see what she'll say.

"Let's do it," Fanny says. "Dog. What a dog."

CHAPTER 44

Elizabeth is now crystal clear. Answering letters is fun. But she wants action.

"Dear Desperate," Elizabeth types, not into a Word document that will go to her editor but into an email message that will go directly to the original sender—from an anonymous Gmail account, of course.

> *Dear Desperate,*
>
> *It's me, Dottie. I've been thinking about you. Not sure the advice I gave you was any good. But I have an idea. Are you serious about your husband—about getting rid of your husband, that is? I can help. No kidding. Hit reply. Send your zip code. And we're in business.*
>
> > *I'm concerned about you,*
> > *Dottie*

Desperate (who in real life really is named Betty) is surprised to find the message when she opens her email. But it's nice to think someone is thinking about her and wants to help. And Ben (not his real name) has gotten worse. He's become so wrapped up in his work that Betty doesn't have a husband anymore. He might as well be dead.

She reads the email again. Could it be a trick of some kind? One of those sting operations she's seen on television? At this point Betty doesn't care. "19133," she types.

Betty gets a response almost instantly. (Elizabeth has been staring at the water, relishing the view, waiting to hear the ping that means there's mail in the box.)

"Oh, hello, Desperate in Philadelphia," Elizabeth types. "Listen to me. I'm going to help you. But you have to do exactly as I say. Take the computer you're reading this on to the Ben Franklin Bridge tomorrow night and throw it in the Schuylkill River. Sounds extreme, I know. But we can't have any evidence of our online connection. Then go to the Package Center on Bainbridge Street the next morning, ask for a delivery in the name of Betty Smith, tracking number 5293-0471-2895-0414. You're going to get away with this. We are. I promise."

Most people wouldn't follow instructions from a total stranger, especially if the instructions involve tossing an expensive computer into a river.

But Betty isn't most people. She's a distraught woman, one who is married to a total creep who has used, humiliated and discarded her, and it's nearly the same to her whether she tosses the computer or herself—and her new perfect size 34C breasts— over the bridge.

A little before midnight, Betty drives to the Ben Franklin Bridge, gets out of her car and walks up the pathway that leads to a deserted span. She throws her laptop over the guardrail. She listens to the splash as it hits the black water beneath. She looks up and around to see if something will happen.

A few minutes pass and nothing does. Betty's stomach tightens.

Is she the dumbest person in the world or what? She just threw her laptop into a river. No wonder Ben left her for Lynette Tart-head or whatever her name is.

Betty picks up the package the next day. Inside she finds a small gray phone, a simple one, without a camera or any doo-dads, just a screen and a keypad that lights up when she touches it. Betty doesn't have anyone to call so she puts the phone on the counter and, from time to time during the day, looks over at it, wondering when or if it might ring.

At dinnertime it does.

"Arrange to take your husband to the Greenwood Beach resort on Cat Island for a romantic four-day Bahamas weekend," says a voice with a strange electronic, recorded sound. The voice suggests some possible vacation dates.

"When you have made the travel arrangements, log on to www.puppyfind.com from a public computer that can't be tied back to you, at a library or FedEx in another town. Say you have a yorkipoo for sale. You will get a call with the rest of your instructions as soon as you do this. Do *not* write them down. Memorize them. When you have, throw this cell phone in the river. Are you serious, Betty? Because I am. Together, we can take care of Ben forever."

Dottie has done her homework.

The recorded message repeats itself, and Betty listens again. A disembodied voice instructing her to do more strange things? Well, it's not as if anyone else is helping her. And she is desperate. She follows all the instructions, then throws the phone in the river.

CHAPTER 45

The view outside Nick's window still excites Fanny's young girl heart: Paris!

Nick, lanky, appealing, dressed, as always, in his crisp white shirt, is pacing. Doing a slalom through a course of French magazines, a stack of his pictures, mismatched shoes, an empty pastry bag. He walks onto the balcony. Clarity brightens his face. "We need to have a hiding place. Somewhere people—even ones who aren't looking for you—won't see you and recognize you from the news photos and missing posters." This sounds crazy to Fanny. But she's game. "For a week at least. It's probably best if we keep you entirely out of sight at first."

Fanny follows with interest. *Really*, she thinks, *everything would have been a lot easier if Rogers' wife had just stayed home where she's supposed to be and Fanny had spent a few days in bed with Rogers and they'd called it a day. Then she'd be back on the campaign trail, not here coming up with screwball plans.*

"We let a '*Where is Fanny?*' hysteria build in the D.C. papers and who knows where else. Then create a few sightings."

Nick looks serious. And there is that stack of pictures.

Could her story be his story? Fanny thinks. *Maybe Nick's a nut job. Or just a lost soul himself.* Fanny wonders why she is listening to him. The answer is: because she is. She likes him. Also she doesn't have lots of other ideas.

"Okay, when do we start?"

Nick's friend Lester knows a camera assistant who has a vacant pied-à-terre near the Eiffel Tower. He moved in with his girlfriend.

Nick checks it out and a day later Fanny is the new resident. Snap. Snap. Nick documents her every move.

It's actually kind of a cool place. At night, if she turns off all the lights and looks out the window, the whole world dissolves and it's just Fanny and the sparkle of la Tour Eiffel, bright lights, la grande cité!

She stays inside, reading, surfing the net, enjoying pain au chocolat and excellent fromage.

As Nick imagined, the American tabloids rev into high gear fast: *Girl Missing? Missing Fanny? Senator Rogers' Wife: My Husband is Not a Fanny Chaser.*

It doesn't take long before "missing girl" stories and old photos of Fanny show up in *Le Monde, Paris Match, People, The Huffington Post.*

Fanny thinks her hair looks good in the school photos the French publications ran; she's sad to see she looks a little fat in the *Paris Match* spread.

CHAPTER 46

Betty awakens with renewed purpose. She's in the kitchen scrambling eggs when Ben walks in.

He sits at his place at the table and Betty delivers his eggs, along with coffee, juice and the paper.

Betty pokes at her eggs while Ben scans the paper. When, at last, he looks up, Betty says, "Darling, let's go away. Me and you. No questions asked about the past. I want to go forward—with you. One chance is all I ask. Four days in the Bahamas. You and me, a lot of sunshine. Let's be together there, and honest, and maybe have a good time too."

"I could use some sunshine," Ben says.

God it would be great to be on Cat Island with Lynette, he thinks, *but hell, she's not offering up a trip. I'll go with Betty, give her the chance she wants, and then goodbye, baby, goodbye, I'm out of here.*

"Wonderful," says Betty.

Two-timing son of a bitch, she thinks as she washes Ben's scrambled egg remains down the garbage disposal. *Next month can't come soon enough.*

CHAPTER 47

Brock hurries to the arrival gate and finds the senator and his wife on the concourse. Today Brock looks like a businessman, not a politician. For one thing, he's wearing a green tie. Political operatives always wear red or blue ones.

"Bonjour," Connie says brightly. She looks particularly frail.

Brock delivers his salutations with the hurried affect Connie expects from him.

"Hello hello. Have a good trip in, Mrs. Rogers? You look exceptional. Nice to see you. Everything is set for you. It will be a wonderful week."

It's hard for Connie to tell if he is hurried because of any actual exigency or if it's just that every word that slips out of Brock's mouth is coated with falsity.

Brock pulls Rogers aside as his wife walks ahead down the concourse, pulling her leather carry-on behind her. He grabs the senator's arm and leans close.

"I got ahold of some local security video on her. Looks like she's hiding out somewhere in the 7th." Brock holds close to Rogers' arm and whispers his discovery into his ear.

"How do you know?" Rogers is processing the information.

"I've got some friends in the security world. But they can only sit on this information for so long. I have to get to her before it leaks. And before your real trouble starts."

CHAPTER 48

Fanny sits in her Eiffel Tower apartment. She looks at the old-fashioned telephone on the wall by the stove. She's called, texted, and emailed her mom. No response.

Nick cautioned her against contacting anyone. But this is her mom! Fanny can't keep her in the dark anymore. Jenny must be going crazy. Maybe she's seen the coverage in the press and flown to Paris to try looking for her? But that doesn't explain why she doesn't answer her phone, doesn't read her email.

Fanny wonders about the whole plan. It looks ridiculous. Much as she likes Nick, his scheme is kind of kooky and far-fetched. The sad fact, though, is that Fanny hasn't got any better ideas.

She picks up the iPad and looks for the latest on the Missing Intern.

A feed from a *Daily Beast* reporter catches her eye: *Could Lovesick Videographer Be Dangerous?*

Is this me? Fanny scrolls down. "A source within Pennsylvania Senator Lee Rogers' campaign revealed today that Fanny Cours became infatuated with the senator and acted erratically in his presence. She was dismissed from the campaign. Another source confirms this description and says the videographer could be 'a dangerous stalker.' "

Fanny bursts into tears. A dangerous stalker! She loves Lee Rogers and he knows it. Who is spreading this garbage about her? No question: Barton Brock. But there's no way he would leak stuff like this without Lee knowing. Fanny feels sick to her stomach, but determined.

She stands up, throws her coat on and storms out the door. Today's the day Lee told that TV reporter he'd be renewing his vows with Connie. She will confront him—and his cheap, demeaning lies—at the Eiffel Tower.

CHAPTER 49

Maybe Fanny would like a bon bon, Lester thinks. He is in line at his favorite boulangerie, two blocks away from the camera assistant's pied-à-terre where Fanny is holed up.

"I'll take one of those," Lester says to the woman behind the counter, pointing to a sugary confection he plans to drop off with Fanny. *When in France*, he thinks.

Bon bon in hand, he approaches Fanny's block when the front door swings open. Who should come out but the lost girl herself? Lester is about to call out to her. But he notices a broad-shouldered man in a tan suit and green tie trailing her from half a block back. Looks like he means business—dirty business.

Lester ducks into a doorway and FaceTimes Nick.

"Nick, Lester here. I'm over at Fanny's place and it looks like some guy is following her. Know who this is?" He turns the phone towards the man in the green tie.

Nick stands at the foot of the Eiffel Tower watching the *Vertigo* crew setting up to film. Barton Brock's image flashes up on Nick's phone screen.

"Yes—I think so. That Brock guy. Could that be him?"

Lester watches as Brock gains on Fanny.

"I gotta go. They're turning the corner," says Lester.

"Hold on," says Nick. But it's too late. The line is dead. Nick looks up to see Hildy and Laurent taking their positions.

The AD calls for silence.

Hildy's robe is pulled off revealing a white silk suit. She turns to face Laurent and the AD yells "Action!"

CHAPTER 50

Lee and Connie Rogers get out of a black Mercedes in front of the Eiffel Tower. Connie is a slip of a woman in her blue wrap dress. Her husband steadies her.

"Are you all right, darling?" He is being especially solicitous.

Connie could not be more all right. Well, she'd be more all right if she didn't have the awful prognosis, but mentally she is as chirpy as a bird, so happy to be here, away from the Washington reporters, away from the awful thoughts—paranoid, anxious, self-hating thoughts—that have plagued her during the last weeks.

"Let's forget all that," says Rogers, reading his wife's mind as long-married spouses sometimes do. "We're away from everything. Let's enjoy ourselves. It's spectacular here. What a day. Just like the day we were first here."

Rogers hugs his wife close.

"Let's go up to the top."

They cross the plaza to the elevators.

A second AD directs them away from the lift. Rogers is surprised to see the AD and the rest of the movie crew crowded around the elevator doors. The set photographer seems to be giving him a long look. "What's going on?" Rogers asks.

"Filming," the second AD replies. "A movie."

"Oh? What's the title?" Rogers asks.

"*Vertigo.*"

"Didn't Hitchcock…?"

"Yes." The AD is impatient. "This is the original French version," he says gruffly.

"I see," Rogers says. "Is the tower closed?"

"No, no. Just portions. You can use any of the other three lifts." He gestures towards a small crowd across the way, near one of the tower's other legs.

"Thanks," says Rogers, taking his wife's arm and steering her past the film crew, towards the crowd of students and tourists lining up for the next elevator.

CHAPTER 51

All is racing and running on the plaza outside the Eiffel Tower. Even the pigeons seem hurried as they skitter on wrinkled feet in clucking pursuit of dirty crumbs.

Fanny darts towards the tower. She is oblivious to Brock's presence, and has no idea he's following her as she crosses the plaza. She quickens her step.

She is focused. It's a bit of a trick to keep the anxiety and the excitement in balance. She rushes past the film unit and gets in line as the elevator in the right-hand leg of the tower returns from the top.

Brock is six or seven tourists behind Fanny in line. Lester is in line too, bringing up the rear, eyeing the back of Brock's head and wondering if he should wait for the next car up or chance riding in the same car together.

Fanny fixes her hair. Tucks a little piece behind her ear and wonders if her lipstick is too much.

The elevator door opens. A family with three school-age kids strolls out. Fanny is impatient. Slowly the line files into the car.

Fanny, who was one of the first to enter, is standing in the back, planted in one corner, looking out at the magnificent view. She still doesn't see Brock and Lester.

Fanny's elevator travels up the tower's girders. Brock keeps his face turned to the view. Lester works his way through the crowded elevator and tries to get a closer look at him.

Nick, having seen the senator head into the other elevator a minute earlier, followed along and now, as the doors open, watches Rogers and his wife, all smiles, walk across the observation platform.

CHAPTER 52

Fanny and her unseen companions, Brock and Lester, approach the top of the tower.

It's windy but bright. Connie and Lee are here, fully here, both of them, in this moment. Gone for the first time in as long as he can remember are the senator's thoughts about policy issues, opposition research, war chests.

Connie is so glad to be with her husband, so glad to be away from the reporters and the pressure and the questions, that she has even forgotten to think what the wind may do to her hair.

The senator and his wife head for the east corner of the tower, where, Connie recalls, Rogers first told her he did not intend to live without her.

What was I wearing on that sunny day? Connie wonders. She is surprised to find that she can't remember.

Rogers takes Connie's hand and they walk to stand at the edge of the railing and behold the view.

Rogers pulls Connie towards him. "Do you remember the last time we were here?"

Connie is all smiles. "Lee, you've got to be kidding. Of course I do."

"Almost thirty years ago," he says.

"To the day. To the hour."

The words are just out of Connie's nicely lipsticked lips when Fanny's elevator arrives. The doors slide open. The passengers file out, slowly.

CHAPTER 53

Nick observes the strange entourage gathering on the observation deck. Lee and Connie are chest to chest, in fleshful embrace as Fanny walks out of the elevator. Rogers leans in and kisses Connie. Nick sees that Fanny is watching and has caught her man, kissing his wife. He sees the paralyzed, deer-in-headlights look on Fanny's face.

She blinks back tears—or is it rage? There is a point where viscera are so powerful that they compress an entire range of feelings—injury, grief, fury—into something that can be mistaken for madness. Nick sees this look on Fanny's face as she watches Lee and Connie. Fanny is no doubt thinking, *Hey! That should be me!* Nick puts his camera to his eye and closes in on them.

Through the lens, Nick sees a man in a tan suit and green tie move up behind Fanny. Barton Brock! The sinister creep who set Elizabeth's and Fanny's lives off course.

Fanny tenses up. She is coiled like a snake and looks like she is about to strike, to confront Rogers, or worse.

Nick watches Brock take this in and move, quietly, towards Fanny.

Fanny, in turn, moves closer to Connie Rogers. It all happens in that funny slow-motion way events unfold in the heat of certain moments. Nick's camera is still trained on Lee and Connie.

Fanny comes into Rogers' view as he, deep in his embrace, stares dreamily into the distance behind Connie's shoulder. He looks aghast.

Nick starts shooting. *Snap. Snap.*

Rogers' face is frozen with something like terror and genuine confusion. Obviously he is too surprised to summon his *Everything-is-fine-Everything-is-under-control-Stand-back-everyone!* senatorial command.

Instead he drops his wife from his grasp. He makes a helpless flailing motion with his arms. His lover! He backs away. Fanny looks confused. What is the blank dead look in his eye?

Fanny reaches one hand out towards him and exclaims, "Lee. It's me. Fanny."

Hearing the voice, Mrs. Rogers turns. She's used to Lee's fans. But in Paris? Too funny!

Brock is fast. He doesn't waste a moment. He springs to action, a regular shot-put move, and shoves Fanny out of the way before Mrs. Rogers locates the voice. Fanny flies over the rail and off the side of the tower. Nick continues shooting in horror. Lester goes after Brock. He wrestles him to the ground. Rogers and his wife watch in a state of semi-shock and disbelief.

Nick, crushed by the ending he has orchestrated, drops his camera to his side and looks over the railing at the dark shape that is Fanny on the plaza below.

CHAPTER 54

The news reports agree with the general consensus that the young girl might have been a stalker, and for the most part celebrate Barton Brock and his heroic reflexes. "Candidate's aide deflects oncoming human projectile," is how one paper puts it. "Protects candidate's wife from harm." Nick's photographs document the event.

Connie finds these reports bewildering. And mortifying.

A stalker? This mixed-up girl with some sort of deranged interest in her husband? How could she ever have thought that Lee would be mixed up with this poor, lost girl?

The events on the tower happened so quickly, Connie barely knew what hit her, or more accurately what Barton Brock kept from hitting her.

There she was, in Lee's arms, Paris and their life together, past and future, glittering before them, Connie reveling in the pure pleasure of having Lee all to herself. She couldn't remember the last time they'd been together, alone and away from the stress of daily life and Lee's work.

But here they were, renewing their vows, standing together, bound by a whole history of children and shared experiences, happy, banal and disappointing, all of it. The awful illness, the jubilant re-elections, all of it mixed up together.

And standing there, she felt they were triumphant over time, together. *This*, thought Connie, as she stood with the wind whipping past them, as she stood with Lee in the Paris air, *this is what marriage is: a history that binds, that offers itself, despite the boredom, loneliness and even the despair that plagues us all, as a reservoir of strength and hope, a bulwark against the world.*

And then Brock—where did he even come from?—bursting out of nowhere and the girl flying over the edge and all the commotion that followed. Connie held tight to Lee's hand as the police rushed her and the rest of the people on the platform downstairs for questioning. Connie had no answers. She'd seen nothing. Understood nothing, except that the moment she'd shared with her husband had been shattered.

She and Lee weren't detained for long. He tucked her into the Mercedes and off they drove to the four-star dinner he'd booked as an anniversary surprise. Her heart was still racing halfway through the meal. She accepted the glass of champagne the waiter offered. Connie's doctors probably wouldn't mind if she had a sip or two, even with the Parkinson's medicines, not on this occasion.

After dinner, she and Lee went back to the hotel as planned and Lee drafted what Connie thinks a lovely letter expressing his regret over the loss of life and counseling all to march forward, to live life to the fullest and in harmony with our best American values.

The next morning, amid the flurry of news coverage, the reaction of the staff is similar to the general reaction, with an element of pride blended in: Barton Brock, one of their own, kept frail Connie Rogers out of harm's way. Too bad a life was lost in the process. *But that videographer? A weird one, no? A stalker, they're saying.*

The flight home is uneventful. In the days that follow, except for a few very bad dreams, Connie thinks little about any of what she and Lee refer to, when necessary, only as "the tower."

The work in Rogers' headquarters hums on until November 8, when Rogers, by a notable margin, handily wins Pennsylvania's senatorial election.

"Another term, another adventure," he tells Brock after his democratic rival's concession speech. "You look tired, Brock. Take some time off. We have a lot of work ahead."

CHAPTER 55

Nick Sculley sorts out his own recent history in the Paris hotel room that once sheltered Fanny. What would he like to tell her now? God. He can't think of a thing. It's all so awful.

"Sorry, kid." That's pretty much the extent of what he'd say if he could. How lame is that. Sorry, kid.

But what else could you say to a bright young girl who threw it all away for junk love with someone who didn't deserve her? Lee Rogers. What a joke. What a bad joke on voters and everyone else. Nick can't even enjoy the good fortune the cataclysm of events has delivered to him.

He told Manny he knew Fanny, explained how she had confided in him when he found her drunk on the Paris Métro.

"You knew that girl? Did you take any pictures of her before the tower? A dozen publishers want her story!"

Nick could barely respond. Great. Yes, he could write about her. And he'd finally get a publisher to publish his pictures. That book might sell. But Fanny was his friend. Her blood still stains the sidewalk outside the Eiffel Tower tourist station. And Brock is on his way to doing who knows what for that creep senator with the high-voltage smile and no apparent principles.

"No way," Nick told Manny.

He leans on the rail of his Paris balcony, slightly soils the sleeve of his starched white shirt on the railing, and tries to make sense of things.

CHAPTER 56

Betty and Ben, nicely depleted from their first day in paradise, retreat to their bungalow. It is white white white. Bougainvillea blooms astoundingly in blinding pink and orange against the side of the little one-story building.

It all seems perfect. And that's deliberate. Betty has been careful to follow to the letter the instructions she received over the cell phone, the one she threw in the river.

Lord how strange this is! thinks Betty, almost forgetting how desperate she is. She replays in her mind the instructions she's received: "Your first night there, put on some romantic music. Do this at seven forty-five."

Betty checks the clock, then plugs her iPhone into the portable speaker system—hotel or bungalow rooms everywhere, even Cat Island, come with them—and presses play. Soft, sensuous music fills the room. Jobim.

Betty tells Ben to get undressed and lie down, face down, under the sheet in the bedroom. She's booked a special massage for the two of them, and the masseuse is on her way. He'll get his first and then they'll swap.

She's thinking: *Oh, he'll get his, all right.*

Special massage? I can go for that, Ben thinks as he puts his head on his forearm and waits.

The recorded voice had instructed Betty to drop Ben's room key in the trashcan in the ladies room beside the lobby. This is just what Betty does after she leaves the bungalow, then heads to the hotel bar at the other end of the main building.

She still finds herself wondering if the whole thing is for real.

The email, the cell phone—those were real. But will a total stranger actually fly to the Bahamas, dig through the trash in the ladies room, find the key, take it to Bungalow 412, and...and... It's hard to believe. Hard to know if she even really, seriously wants it to be true. No, that's not right: she wants it. She really does.

Meanwhile, even if the whole thing is a big fat farce, it's kind of fun. The sea air is pleasant; the hotel and the beaches are pretty. Betty goes to the hotel bar and orders herself a drink. She lifts the glass and toasts herself. "Here's to the end of Ben and his cheating heart," she says to herself as she inhales the drink in one big gulp. Then she orders another. She checks her watch. It's 8:09.

"Oh my goodness," she says to the bartender, "how much do I owe you? I have to run. It's after eight."

"Going to the show?" the bartender asks, meaning the duo in the piano bar covering Broadway classics; they go on at 8:15 and 10:15.

"Uh-huh." That should burn the time nicely into his mind.

But the instructions were very specific; establish an airtight alibi. Airtight. Okay, thinks Betty. She picks up her drink, paper umbrella and all, and carries it over to a table where a nicely dressed middle-aged man is sitting with his young lady friend.

And then she falls over their table, spilling her drink all over the older man's lap.

"You old coot," she shouts. "Look at you. And look what you made me do!"

The man looks startled.

Betty lifts a water glass off the table and tosses its contents in the man's face.

Two waiters rush up and start mopping up the table and the man, who asks that they please remove Betty from his sight.

Politely, one of the waiters takes her arm and leads her to the door.

"Forgive me," Betty whispers in the waiter's ear, "I'm a little tipsy and I didn't like the look of that fellow. Too old to be carrying on with a young woman, don't you think? It's okay, I'm out of here. Nearly 8:15 isn't it? Yes sir! Thanks for the escort."

Betty thinks she is a very good actress.

The waiter thinks, *Whatever they're paying me here, it's not enough.*

Inside Bungalow 412, Ben opens his eyes when he hears the bedroom door open. He feels the light breeze from the ceiling fan on his bare skin, feels the old ache in his balls.

He hears the masseuse approaching. Peeking to one side, he sees a tall woman with short dark hair in a light white sheath dress.

"Close your eyes," the woman says without turning around.

Eyes closed, Ben hears the masseuse moving around. From the sound of it, she's going through her handbag, probably for oils or whatever.

He thinks of Lynette. He loves the way she makes him feel. She knows just how to touch him.

"Hello," says the masseuse, "I have something very special for you." Her voice is low and smoky-sounding.

Ben smiles. "What would you like me to do?"

"Just relax. We'll start with your back. Must be sore after the long flight, no?"

Ben is confused. The masseuse sounds sexy. She has a familiar—naughty—intonation. But he can't tell what is going on. Sexed-up visions of Lynette drift into his mind. Maybe he has imagined erotic connotations that aren't here.

He enjoys the feel of flesh on his shoulder. The masseuse has wet her fingertips with sweet-smelling oil and it is warm and transporting as it sinks into his skin.

The masseuse presses her hands down the surface of his back. The oil melts around her fingers. Ben is conscious of a vague stirring in his loins.

He listens as she reaches with one hand for what he assumes is more oil, mmmm, smells like...what is that? Flowers? Citrus...?

A volt of electric heat burns through Ben's left lung. His head lurches upward. "What the fuck?" he's about to yell but the current searing through his neck chokes the words before they get anywhere near his mouth, which fast fills with the hot iron taste of burnt blood.

Elizabeth wrestles the blade out and drives it into Ben's dark heart, again and again, four times.

Hard work too. The body is a lot stronger than you'd think.

Elizabeth leans back to avoid the blood gush, then takes off her dress, uses it to wipe the handle of the knife, steps into the shower, dries quickly and, exchanging her stained dress for a clean one she has in her bag, Elizabeth dresses quickly and lets herself out the bungalow.

"Goodbye, Ben, pig," she says, on her way out the door.

Carefully following instructions, Betty returns to the corridor outside Bungalow 412 after Elizabeth has finished her business inside.

She has called in an order for wine and cheese from room service. The delivery man is approaching as Betty heads down the long path towards the bungalow. And then, quite deliberately, Betty crashes straight into the waiter and knocks a bottle off his cart. "I'm so sorry I'm late. I didn't want to disappoint my husband." She acts, and in fact is, flustered.

"That's all right, madam," says the waiter. "It's pretty dark out here. Is this your bungalow? I have room service for you."

"Absolutely," she says. "Let's see if my husband wants anything else."

Betty is agitated and has to try several times to get her card key in the slot. She's not sure what she'll find inside the bungalow. What if everything went wrong? What if everything went exactly as planned? Betty is genuinely unsure which is worse. Her heart thumps under her dress.

Betty gets the card in at last and hears the lock open. The waiter follows her in, starts unloading the cart's contents while she heads into the bedroom. It is quiet for a second. Then Betty screams. A completely genuine blood-curdling cry. *"Oh my god. Please help me! Get a doctor! My husband! He's been stabbed! Help!"*

The scene inside the room will haunt the waiter for years: the bed is soaked in blood. The naked corpse is bright red with it. The blade is buried five inches deep in his back.

The waiter reaches for the hotel phone. He can barely speak. "Bungalow 412. Help! A man. Stabbed. Get a doctor. Fast. Yes! Bungalow 412! Mr. Brock. Yes. Mr. Barton Brock."

Time collapses like a telescope, and the waiter is unsure how long it takes before there is a clamor of footfalls outside the door. He takes his leave, sick to his stomach, pushing the room service cart as the manager and someone who must be a doctor rush into the room.

Squeak squeak. The cart wheel is noisy but the waiter hears the manager say to that nice woman outside the room, "I'm so sorry, Mrs. Brock. So, so sorry."

CHAPTER 57

Dear Dottie:

I didn't think you'd do it.

Don't get me wrong, I'm glad you did. I'm grateful that you did. But it's left me in limbo and I need your help. Not help — no more help like that! Just advice. The sort of help you usually give.

Barton's death (now that he's gone I can use his real name, Barton B. Brock —

Elizabeth's eyes widen. Her breath stops. She looks again.

…..Barton B. Brock…..

She does a double-take. *Barton B. Brock —* yes, that's definitely what it says! A blast of surprise and great satisfaction rises in her chest as she reads on.

…(now that he's gone I can use his real name, Barton B. Brock) was a big, horrible shock — so much blood, the knife, the doctor who took him out. But that wasn't the worst part.

Afterwards, I was alone in the hotel room, before they moved me. That was so awful. I could see the blood every-where. So I closed my eyes. And thought about what had happened in our lives together — the baby I'd wanted, the life Barton promised and dangled in front of me, the cruel sport he made of me, gullible me, foolish stupid me.

Why did I think he would end things with that girl and come home, to me and our life, the one we made together? I fell for every one of his cheap lies. I'd been had. Cheated. What a reptile. Why did I think I needed Barton to get on?

*Will I ever get that sight out of my mind: the wet wall and
the bloody sheets, Barton's body a big splatter of red wet
goo?*

*But that isn't the worst part either. The worst part—the
part that chills my blood—is that, oh gosh, it's horrible to
say, Dottie, the worst part is—this can't be right; it must be
wrong—the most horrible scary thing is that I feel, well, just
fine. Kind of pretty. Better than I have in years.*

*Even that newly widowed man, the pastor's shy brother,
remarked on how well I have been holding up. "You're just a
remarkable creature," he said.*

*With my frilly new underthings (a pick-me-up treat I bought
for myself) I was even thinking maybe I would have "tea" with
the pastor's brother. Yep. He came straight out and invited
me for tea after church on Sunday, and some mischief, I think
he said.*

*But, you know, Dottie, I'm feeling so good about things.
Why wreck it? Maybe I won't have "tea" with him after all.
He's handsome and shy and all but what the devil does he
think he's doing with his poor wife so recently gone—her
body's practically still warm.*

*What do you think? Should I talk to someone, a psychiatrist
or something? It doesn't seem right to be feeling so…good.
And where, at my age, do I get off rebuffing advances from
decent churchgoing fellows?*

What do you think? Please help.

Feeling Groovy

Elizabeth nearly whoops with glee. It will take a while for
her to fully register the strange good fortune fate delivered to
her: to make two wrongs right with just one knife (and several
strong blows).

Feeling Groovy indeed!

Elizabeth bites her lip, stifling all but one peal of jubilant laughter, and gets to the business at hand, the astounding, unanswered letter.

Dear Feeling Groovy,

   So happy to hear you are enjoying yourself. Put those frilly underthings back on, prance about, let it rip.

   As for your pastor's brother, you tell me: Is the sky green? Is the pope Jewish? What do you think, Betty, are snakes necessary?

Don't Let the Mystery End Here.
Try More Great Books From
HARD CASE CRIME!

Hard Case Crime brings you gripping, award-winning crime fiction
by best-selling authors and the hottest new writers in the field.
Find out what you've been missing:

BRAINQUAKE
by **SAMUEL FULLER**

For more than ten years, Paul Page was the perfect bagman.
But that ended the day he saw a beautiful Mob wife become a
Mob widow. Now Paul is going to break every rule he's lived by
to protect the woman he loves—even if it means he might be
left holding the bag...

In a career that spanned half a century, Samuel Fuller wrote
and directed classic movies that inspired filmmakers as varied
as Steven Spielberg, Martin Scorsese, Francis Ford Coppola,
Jean-Luc Godard, Jim Jarmusch, Wim Wenders, and Quentin
Tarantino. He also wrote unforgettable novels such as the noir
classic *The Dark Page*—and this book, his last, which was never
previously published in the English language.

Raves for Samuel Fuller:

"A great, great, great storyteller."
— Martin Scorsese

"Personal, hard-hitting, idiosyncratic...
Everything was about storytelling, the great yarn."
— Quentin Tarantino

Available now at your favorite bookstore.
For more information, visit
www.HardCaseCrime.com